"It's twelve nights, Poppy, not a lifetime."

"Twelve nights?" she groaned. "You're coming for the whole time? You never come for the whole time."

"Things are different this year." He hesitated. "My father needs me."

"Twelve nights," she said after a moment, as Adrastos cut through the streets of Henrikburg, the suburbs morphing from bohemian to more upmarket frontages. She'd never been to his house, but the moment he turned into the street, she could pick which was his—from the beefed-up security presence and hordes of paparazzi waiting on the street.

He swore, pulling the car to a stop on the side of the road.

"Well, Poppy? Moment of truth. If you're going to do this, now would be an excellent chance to put on a united front for the media."

"I told you, I need to think..."

"Neither of us has the luxury of time."

He was right.

"Damn it," she groaned, lifting a shaking hand to her forehead. "Fine, I agree, in principle, to be your fake girlfriend, but we still need to work out the details."

"I'm open to negotiations."

Clare Connelly was raised in small-town Australia among a family of avid readers. She spent much of her childhood up a tree, Harlequin book in hand. Clare is married to her own real-life hero, and they live in a bungalow near the sea with their two children. She is frequently found staring into space—a surefire sign she is in the world of her characters. She has a penchant for French food and ice-cold champagne, and Harlequin novels continue to be her favorite-ever books. Writing for Harlequin Presents is a long-held dream. Clare can be contacted via clareconnelly.com or on her Facebook page.

Books by Clare Connelly

Harlequin Presents

Emergency Marriage to the Greek
Pregnant Princess in Manhattan
The Boss's Forbidden Assistant

Passionately Ever After...

Cinderella in the Billionaire's Castle

The Cinderella Sisters

Vows on the Virgin's Terms
Forbidden Nights in Barcelona

The Long-Lost Cortéz Brothers

The Secret She Must Tell the Spaniard
Desert King's Forbidden Temptation

Visit the Author Profile page
at Harlequin.com for more titles.

Clare Connelly

TWELVE NIGHTS IN THE PRINCE'S BED

Recycling programs for this product may not exist in your area.

ISBN-13: 978-1-335-59201-9

Twelve Nights in the Prince's Bed

For questions and comments about the quality of this book, please contact us at CustomerService@Harlequin.com.

Harlequin Enterprises ULC
22 Adelaide St. West, 41st Floor
Toronto, Ontario M5H 4E3, Canada
www.Harlequin.com

Printed in U.S.A.

TWELVE NIGHTS IN THE PRINCE'S BED

CHAPTER ONE

THIS WAS THEIR tenth shared birthday party, their tenth year as best friends, and despite what she'd lost in life Poppy Henderson looked out at the room filled with guests and felt grateful. What would her life have been like without Her Royal Highness Princess Eleanor Aetos and the whole Aetos family in it?

After her parents had died, she'd thought she'd never know this kind of contentment again. She'd thought she'd never know the love of family, the sense of belonging, but her parents' best friends, who just so happened to be the King and Queen of Stomland, had wrapped their arms around Poppy despite their own heavy sense of grief after the death of their oldest son, and never let go. They'd treated her like a daughter from the beginning, and their love had helped Poppy to heal. She was so grateful to them, there was nothing she wouldn't do for the King and Queen.

As for the royal children, Eleanor had become a sister to Poppy instantly and Eleanor's brother Adrastos…well, that relationship was a little harder to define. Up until she was twenty-one she would have described him as a brother of sorts, albeit five years older and a little serious and cool. But he'd been kind as well, and had never once acted as though he minded Poppy's intrusion into their family.

Of their own volition, her eyes drifted across the room, finding him easily as they always did, and her heart kicked up a gear, her stomach tightening uncomfortably at just the sight of him. They'd barely spoken since that night, Ellie's and Poppy's twenty-first birthdays. Had it really been three years ago? Her skin flushed with memories she tried not to think about, the confusion of having someone she'd regarded almost as a brother draw her into his arms and kiss her until she was intimately aware of him as a man, a man she desired very, very much…

The memory she tried desperately to forget, because it was so incendiary and confusing she couldn't make sense of it. The way his hands had pulled her close that night, held her against his hard, taut body, his eyes challenging her for a moment before he'd dropped his head and his lips had met hers. Sparks of desire had ignited in Poppy's bloodstream and she'd finally *understood* what lust was. She'd lost herself in those moments, moments that had seemed to stretch and take over all of time for Poppy. He'd kissed her and she'd almost forgotten who and where she was, until a noise had broken through the spell and they'd pulled apart, each as shocked as the other, eyes locked as they'd tried to make sense of the madness that had overtaken them.

'That shouldn't have happened. I'm sorry.'

His apology had surprised her, because Adrastos wasn't the kind of man who made mistakes. He was never in the wrong—even the media had said as much: the papers were constantly running stories celebrating Adrastos's victories. Had the kiss been wrong? Reality had sliced through Poppy quickly enough and she'd remembered the truth of their situation, her loyalty to his parents, the fact they'd been raised since her parents' deaths almost as siblings. But *not* siblings, she hastily comforted herself.

Poppy stared at Adrastos now as if she were a starving person led to a banquet, while Adrastos was distracted enough for her to be able to take full advantage.

Where Eleanor had inherited her mother's blonde hair and slight figure, Adrastos was a throwback to his ancient ancestors, warriors shaped in the cradle of civilisation, with those broad shoulders and muscular arms honed by his pursuit of all sports, but particularly car racing and rowing—she remembered him waking early and taking to the Mediterranean, training with his crew until he was covered in perspiration. He would return to the palace smelling of sea salt and power.

Days after their kiss, it had been abundantly clear Adrastos had put it completely from his mind. He had been back to his usual tricks, pictured in the nation's papers with a beautiful actress from Germany. A week after that, it had been a Spanish model. Six weeks later, a world-famous Swiss athlete. Adrastos—a renowned bachelor—had simply got on with his life, just as it had been before The Kiss. So why couldn't Poppy get him out of her head even then? Why couldn't she date another guy? Try to find that same spark she'd felt when Adrastos had kissed her?

Locked in conversation with one of his cousins, Adrastos shifted slightly, his eyes moving quickly and landing directly on Poppy, almost as if he knew where she was standing, almost as if…

She put a stop to that thought, too. There was no way he'd been watching her.

Their eyes met and the same sparks that had ignited her bloodstream three years earlier were back, fierce and out of control.

On the night of her twenty-first birthday, quite out of nowhere, Poppy had been awakened with feelings she hadn't known existed. And she'd liked it. But ever since, that side of her had been dormant, unexplored, unknown. Her virginity was something she couldn't understand. It hadn't been a conscious choice. Before the kiss, she'd been busy at university, working very hard to live up to her parents' academic successes, and to make the royal couple proud. And afterwards? The thought of any other man turned her body to ice. It had been easy not to date, not to flirt, not to desire. But now, at twenty-four, in the same room as Adrastos, her body was charged with a billion tiny sparks, more energy than all the stars in the universe.

Perhaps it was the last disastrous date she'd attempted. A month earlier, she'd let Eleanor set her up with a friend of a friend. A man she'd liked. Enjoyed the company of. But when he'd tried to kiss her goodnight, she'd felt nausea rising in her chest and had known that if his lips touched hers, she'd have vomited over their shoes. Mortified, she'd recoiled, made an excuse and bolted inside her townhouse, feeling broken and stupid and wondering what the hell was wrong with her.

Like a sinkhole, Adrastos drew her attention back, and there it was: fizzing in her veins, a sense of certainty and need, a reckless desire to understand what had happened between them all those years ago, to understand why he had been able to flood her with desire where no one else had. Was she simply not a sexual person? Had she mistaken her reactions to Adrastos that night? Or would she feel the same way now, if they were to kiss once more…?

Swiping another champagne from a passing tray, she took three generous sips before clutching the glass a little too tightly in her hands and sashaying across the room, her pulse racing as she drew closer to Adrastos, her heart thumping so hard it jumped out of its usual position in her chest and lodged somewhere in the vicinity of her throat.

But surely this was too late? Three years? How many women had he been with since? Would he even remember?

And just as that question struck her in the face, Adrastos turned once more, their eyes locked, and the world stopped spinning. Poppy's mouth went dry and nothing else mattered. Spurred on by the fact it was her birthday, by just the right amount of champagne, and by the fact that earlier today she'd accepted a job in the Netherlands that would see her moving from Stomland and starting afresh, she inched forward, ever so slightly.

She had to know, to understand…to feel alive again… Her breath caught in the very back of her throat and when she spoke, the words tumbled out almost too fast.

'Do you have a moment, Your Highness?' The title might have seemed strange but even though they'd spent so much time together, certain formalities still tended to be observed, particularly when they were around others.

Adrastos's eyes narrowed almost imperceptibly, and Poppy's nerves were frayed, the possibility that he might say 'no' was real and suddenly very scary. But a moment later, he dipped his head, a curt expression on his face but agreement conveyed by the subtle gesture.

'What is it?' He took a small step away from the group he'd been standing with.

Poppy again squeezed the glass in her hand, surprised in the back of her mind that it didn't shatter completely. He was so handsome. So familiar and so completely strange all at once. Adrenalin made her aware of every vertebra in her back.

'Can we speak somewhere more private?'

His Adam's apple shifted but otherwise his face didn't move, didn't betray a single response to that question. After a beat, he nodded. 'There's a balcony. Do you have a coat?'

Poppy looked over her shoulder, waved indistinctly towards the makeshift cloakroom, over on the other side of the penthouse, with dozens of revellers in between.

'You may use mine,' he said, so Poppy's eyes skittered to his and she had to dig her fingernails into her palms to hold her resolve firm.

'I'm fine. This won't take long.' But even as she said it, she felt a little throb of excitement, the creaking open of a door to a world of possibilities she'd never before contemplated. She was being silly. Egged on by champagne and curiosity, by the fantasies that kiss had spawned when he'd taken a perfectly content yet inexperienced twenty-one-year-old and shown her just a glimpse of what her body was capable of feeling.

He didn't touch her, but as they cut through the room she felt his nearness like a caress and her whole body responded, goosebumps lifting, her stomach twisting with the realisation that she was about to be alone with him for the first time in years.

It was impossible to walk anywhere with Adrastos and not acknowledge the way people watched him. She saw heads turn, women appraise, men react with respect. A blade of doubt pushed its way into her thoughts, so she knew she had to do this quickly and get it over with.

At the doors to the balcony, he stopped abruptly, turning to look at her with an expression that could best be described as doubt, his eyes raking over her, almost as if he'd never seen her before, as if he wanted to say, 'Are you sure?'

In response to the unasked question, Poppy tilted her chin and held his gaze with a defiance she wasn't quite sure she felt.

A moment later, the Crown Prince opened the door, and a blast of ice-cold wind rushed in at the same time they stepped out, the gentle din of the party silenced the moment the door clicked shut behind them.

Poppy loved Stomland.

When she'd first come here, her heart had been broken, shattered by her parents' shocking deaths, and she'd recognised in the royal family kindred spirits—in many ways, but particularly in their shared state of grief, having lost their oldest son just months before her parents. They told Poppy, many times over the years, how her arrival had helped to mend their family, to make them feel a little closer to whole, and it was a sentiment Poppy shared.

'Well, Poppy?'

She almost flinched at the cool tone of his question. Before the kiss, they hadn't been close. Not like her and Ellie. They were best friends as well as sisters in spirit. Adrastos had always been a step removed, busy and important, carrying the weight of the world on his shoulders. But they'd at least been friendly. He'd been protective, just as he was with Ellie. She'd been in awe of him, intimidated by his overwhelming strength and masculinity, but there'd never been this kind of awkwardness, this skin-tingling awareness.

Now they were here, alone, the questions she wanted to ask seemed insurmountable to speak.

Silence fell, a silence in which Poppy was aware of absolutely everything. His breathing, the smell of the salt water, the sound of distant traffic, his aftershave, the cool night air, heavy with the promise of Christmas, just around the corner. They hadn't been this close, alone, since the kiss, and it was impossible not to feel ghost memories of that touch flicking over her skin. Was he thinking of it too?

'Poppy?' The sharpness to her name had her eyes darting to his, her heart racing. 'What did you want from me?'

It was a curious phrasing. Not, 'What do you want to discuss with me?' Somehow, his choice of words was so much more provocative. She took another gulp of champagne, eyes closed, letting it explode into her belly.

'I'm—' She opened her eyes, stared at him, and lost sense of everything. Whatever they'd been before her twenty-first and anything that had happened since didn't matter. The stars overhead seemed to wink down at them, giving Poppy their blessing, or, at the very least, their encouragement. Maybe it was a devilish idea, maybe she'd regret it, but tonight, Poppy was filled with a need that only Adrastos could meet. She didn't want to think about the consequences.

That kiss on the night of her twenty-first had been just a flash. A few passionate seconds she'd replayed over and over and over so many times the memory was in danger of getting static cracks through it from overuse. A fresh taste of Adrastos, a secret, forbidden kiss, just for this one night...

Time seemed to slow almost to a stop. She was conscious of the very atmosphere that wrapped around them, the cool winter's night, the sparkle of the stars overhead, the sound of the ocean lapping against boats in the distance, and then, Adrastos. All of him. Right there, within easy touching distance.

She licked her lower lip quickly, mouth dry, throat thick. His eyes dropped to her mouth and her heart accelerated so she thought it might hop out of her chest. It was now or never.

'What I want,' she said, slowly, but with steel underpinning those words, a challenge in each syllable, 'is for you to kiss me.' She moved closer, so her breath fanned his cheek. 'But this time,' she almost purred, 'I don't want you to stop.'

Adrastos felt the boundaries of his world tighten around his body, making it impossible to breathe, to think, to see anything besides this damned woman, this vexatious, tempting, beautiful woman. When had that happened? She'd been a teenager at first, just like his sister. The pair of them so silly, always giggling and whispering secrets. He'd looked on them both with fond indulgence. He'd never thought of Poppy as a *woman*, until her twenty-first birthday party, when he'd walked into the garden marquee that had been erected in the grounds of the palace and seen—not just a woman, but a deity. A goddess. Stunningly beautiful, untouchable and entirely transformed. Suddenly, all their conversations over the years, all their shared stories, everything he knew about Poppy, had shifted and morphed and he'd wanted to *really* know her, beyond the words they'd exchanged. He'd wanted her in a way that he hadn't even fully understood. He'd had plenty of experience with women, but he'd never wanted another human being in the way he wanted Poppy. It went way beyond sex. He'd seen her and wanted to make her his on some elemental level.

The need to possess her had terrified him. He'd spent the entire night trying to avoid her, to tamp down on those unwelcome feelings, and he'd almost succeeded. He'd almost won the war, but then she'd walked past him, quite distracted by a conversation with his mother, and Adrastos had fallen under her spell. Her fragrance, so sweet and sensual, had called to him, and when he'd found her alone, in the rose garden—one of her favourite spots—he'd known the war was far from over: it was no longer in his grasp to win.

If a waiter hadn't walked past that night and dropped a glass, rousing Adrastos to his sanity, he would have made love to Poppy then and there, amongst the roses.

But that had been three years ago. He'd run so hard from that night, that unfamiliar moment that had completely lacked Adrastos's trademark control, when he'd kissed a woman he'd been told to think of as his damned sister! He had no right desiring her. He had no right to kiss her. Any other woman, he thought with a grimace. Adrastos had made no effort to hide his lifestyle from the press. If anything, he'd relished that reputation.

Having been lauded as 'The Perfect Prince' since Nicholas's death, in one aspect of his life, at least, he didn't feel like a treacherous usurper. He couldn't change his traits, those inbuilt leadership instincts that did indeed make him an excellent prince. Nor could he change the fact that Nicholas had been, in many ways, unsuitable for the life for which he'd been born. He'd been quiet, academic, timid and naturally shy, every public outing a torture for the oldest sibling, where Adrastos cared so little for anyone's opinion of him that he'd not been bothered by any engagement whatsoever.

But he hated the comparisons.

He hated that at times there'd almost been a sense of joy at Adrastos's promotion to heir—never mind that it had come about through the death of his much-loved brother.

Was it any wonder he'd lashed out in the one area of his life that was beyond the control of anyone? While his parents desperately wanted him to settle down and marry, to have royal heirs of his own, Adrastos delighted in showing everyone they were wrong about him—at least a little. He wasn't The Perfect Prince. Not as perfect as Nicholas would have been, because surely Nicholas would have married by now, had he lived.

Poppy made a little noise, a husky exhalation, and she was pulling back, ever so slightly, so his gaze narrowed, his pulse grew louder in his ears and he knew he had seconds to act—or not act, which would be far smarter.

That night, he'd kissed her because he'd wanted her, and he'd pretended it had been just like with any of the women he met in bars or at parties. But this was Poppy. There were layers between them that complicated things. His parents viewed her as a daughter. She had no family besides *his* family. He couldn't take her to bed then forget about her. It was messy and Adrastos didn't do messy.

And yet, even just the thought of kissing her had his groin tightening, his arousal straining against the fabric of his trousers, so he was intimately aware of every inch of his manhood, the powerful need for Poppy compressing the walls of his world even further.

'Listen, Poppy…'

She lifted a finger, pressing it to his lips. 'I don't want to listen,' she murmured. 'I really, really don't want to talk about this. For three years I've wondered what the heck happened between us, and I've wondered why you stopped. I've never understood why all of a sudden we were kissing, and then we weren't, but I've had time to reflect on the whole kissing side of things and I liked it. So I want you to kiss me. Again.'

'And not to stop,' he growled, and despite his mind knowing this was an utterly *terrible* idea, that things were far more complicated than she believed, his hand lifted and pressed to her hip, holding her there, and his body was suddenly so close that they were pressed together.

'Not to stop,' she agreed with a small nod and a tilt of her head so her face was close to his and they were staring at each other. He felt as though he might tumble off the edge of the balcony if she kept looking at him like that.

'It was right to stop that night,' he said, as if he needed to grab a lifeline.

'Was it? Why?' There was an intensity to her question and he was reminded of how razor sharp her mind was, how impressive her intelligence. It was one of the first things he'd noticed about her, all those years ago, when she'd arrived in Stomland as a shell-shocked orphan and he'd felt an instant desire to protect her from any more harm. But even broken by the loss of her parents, she'd been insatiably curious and unabashed with her curiosity.

He compressed his lips and expelled a sharp breath. 'Because you're like a sister to me.'

She made a scoffing noise he regrettably found irresistible.

'A sister? Really?'

No, not really. He sighed again. 'Poppy—'

'Tell me you don't want to kiss me,' she challenged directly, and he was grateful for the darkness on the balcony, and the fact she wouldn't be able to see the tell-tale part of his anatomy that showed just how badly he wanted what she was suggesting. But then, whether by accident or design, she swayed forward, and brushed against his arousal. The moment they connected, her eyes widened and her lips parted on a soft exhalation. There was no longer any denying it. There was no longer a war to wage.

'It's a mistake,' he groaned, but he wasn't sure if she heard: the words were buried in the kiss, in the swift, urgent claiming of her mouth, in the beginning of something he wasn't sure he could control but that he could no longer fight. Hell, it was a mistake, but so was the kiss on Poppy's twenty-first. He'd simply have to live with the consequences in the morning. And in between now and then? He intended to enjoy every damned moment.

CHAPTER TWO

HE'D KISSED HER once before and it had rocked her world, shaken it to the very foundations, but this was something else. Something entirely different. She saw now that his first kiss had been *chaste*, if such a word could be applied to a moment that had switched everything on inside her and made her fully aware of her desires and needs as a woman. But this was different.

This was so raw, so real, so visceral. One hand came behind her back, pulling her hard against him, and his mouth took hers with a rush of desperate hunger, his lips separating hers, his tongue pushing into her mouth as if he wanted to taste every inch of her. She whimpered because it was so incredibly overwhelming, because she felt as if she were drowning, and there was no saviour in sight. She lifted her hand to the back of his head, tangling her fingers in his hair, making a small moaning sound that was swallowed by their kiss.

Desire flashed through her, heavy, hot, urgent, so now she didn't hear the ocean or see the stars, she felt only the tightening of her nipples against the fine lace of her bra, and the warmth between her legs, and the way her stomach was twisting, wanting, needing more.

She didn't ever want this kiss to end. She knew it would lead to complications, but his passion was a drug and she was high on it. Rational thought was no longer possible.

Pressing up onto the tips of her toes, so her breasts crushed against his chest, her body moulded to his, she felt the full force of his arousal and almost pulled back, because it was so confronting and real, such undeniable proof that he was awash with the same desire she was.

Something, somewhere, snapped through the waves of eroticism to steal Poppy's focus, and Adrastos was aware of it too. They both pulled away, staring at each other, chests heaving. Adrastos looked around, frowning.

It had been a flash of light. Lightning? The air smelled of salt and thunder; a storm had been forecast for the following day.

It had also been a wake-up call she desperately didn't want to hear; she couldn't have history repeat itself! The last time, they'd stopped because there'd been a sudden noise, and she'd always lamented that, and wondered what would have been if they'd kept exploring, kept kissing, kept tasting… Staring up at him, she knew the hammer was about to drop, that he would walk away from this and leave her and all her fantasies for the next few years would be fed by those wild, passionate moments of abandon.

'We shouldn't do this,' he said with a shake of his head, but he continued to hold her tight.

Disappointment seared Poppy.

'Anyone could walk out here and see.'

Her heart lifted. She felt as though she were on the fastest roller coaster in the world. His eyes pinned hers as if he was trying to wade through the madness, to find his way back to the shores of sanity. She held her breath, incapable of speaking, too scared to say anything that might shatter the moment.

'Come with me.'

The words were issued like a command, ringing with his trademark authority, the same authority she'd been aware of when she'd first come to live at the palace in Stomland as a heartbroken fourteen-year-old. Eleanor had been a balm to her soul, but nineteen-year-old Adrastos, home for the weekend from military college, had been something else entirely. She'd quickly learned that the sun and moon revolved around him. Not just because he was the heir to this small, rich country, but because he had been born as a true king amongst men—second in line to the throne until his older brother's death, but Adrastos had always been possessed of qualities that made him rare and impressive. Confident, fiercely intelligent, unfairly handsome, educated, strong and athletic, he had been like some kind of god, and to be in the same room as him was to be aware of his gifts. She saw it again and again—the way people were awed by him, totally cast under his spell, just by being near him.

He drew her closer, hand on her back, guiding her across the balcony, every step taking them further away from the party, towards their own intimate celebration. It was a large penthouse, and they walked around the corner of the balcony before reaching a door. With one last, piercing look at Poppy's face, Adrastos pushed the door inwards and gently ushered her inside, the hand on the small of her back almost the only reason she could remain standing.

He flicked on the lights as he shut the door and locked it, offering privacy in what was a sumptuous bedroom. Poppy spun to face him now, dislodging his hand and jacket, which she'd worn loosely draped over her shoulders. It dropped to the ground without her realising it, because she couldn't quite believe what was happening.

A twenty-four-year-old virgin, in a bedroom with the Prince she'd secretly fantasised about for years…

Happy birthday, Poppy.

But this wasn't wise. It was a terrible idea. They'd both regret it.

Or would they? She wouldn't. She knew she wouldn't. In the same way she'd held those memories of their first encounter, sleeping with Adrastos would be another memory. A much, much better memory. And she'd no longer be a virgin… It was something that had niggled at the back of her mind for a long time. She was aware how out of step with her contemporaries she was. It hadn't been intentional. She'd honestly started to think she was just very non-sexual. Only, it turned out, Adrastos seemed to be the only man who could stir her to this kind of fever pitch. Why on earth would she even think about squandering that opportunity?

And if anyone found out?

Adrastos's family were all she had. They'd taken her in rather than letting her awful aunt raise her. Poppy had been so incredibly grateful that they'd fought for her, that they'd brought Poppy to live with them. They'd always gone out of their way to make sure Poppy felt welcome, but, at the end of the day, she wasn't their child. She wasn't really family. They needed Adrastos to follow through with his royal duties. His penchant for sleeping with anything in a skirt was a source of great pain for the King and Queen, and even to Eleanor. So if they learned Poppy had become one of his women? How could they fail to feel betrayed by that?

It would change everything.

Poppy couldn't lose them, too. She couldn't—wouldn't—do anything to upset them, to make them think she'd taken advantage of her place in their lives.

She prevaricated but whatever hesitations she had abruptly disappeared the moment Adrastos began to unbutton his shirt, slowly but determinedly, eyes on her the whole time so she felt as though he saw all the way through her, and she shivered.

Because she wanted him to see her. She wanted this.

It could never be more than this night. She wouldn't risk her place in his family by wanting more—she knew the boundaries. Honestly, Poppy didn't know if she'd survive losing the love of his parents and sister, not after all she'd already lost. Plus, she wasn't a total sadist. Wanting more than one night from Adrastos would be like wanting to sprout wings and fly. One day, he'd give up his bachelor lifestyle, but probably not for many, many years.

'Adrastos…' Her voice was a husky plea, an incantation of some ancient magic, a promise, a pledge.

He stopped unbuttoning his shirt, eyes meeting hers, and then he lifted his hand, holding it outwards. Poppy was just inches away. One single step closed the distance. She stared at his hand a moment, feeling the enormity of what he was asking, then put her own in it. A tremble ran the length of her spine at their connection. Her soul spun.

He was Ellie's brother.

She'd seen him as off-limits for years. To touch him now with freedom, to feel his warmth against her skin, set something going inside her that she almost couldn't bear. Her knees knocked and her stomach flipped.

'You do it.'

Another command.

At her look of uncertainty, he gestured to his shirt. Her veins were filled with a tsunami of blood. She took one more step, then, with fingers that weren't quite steady, began to unfasten the remaining buttons.

He smelled so good up close. Alpine and masculine, with whisky undertones making her belly do somersaults. She breathed in deeply, wanting more of him. She leaned closer, letting her face drift towards his now naked chest, inhaling his fragrance, her lips tingling with a desire to kiss and to taste.

He drew in a deep breath, so his chest moved, his skin just millimetres from her mouth now.

Poppy held back a groan, swallowing it in her mouth, swallowing hard. Reality seemed so far away, but if she was dreaming—again—then she didn't want to wake up.

Her hands pushed the shirt from his body completely, letting it fall to the floor, and her eyes sought his, trying to reconcile this version of Adrastos with the one she'd known for so many years. The heir to the throne, the 'older brother' figure.

'Are you sure about this?' she asked uncertainly, because she couldn't bear it if he changed his mind later. She needed to know. She needed a guarantee that this was going to happen.

'What do you think?' His eyes were hooded, his handsome face tanned, with a slight colouring to his cheekbones.

She lifted her slender shoulders in a half-shrug. 'I don't know.'

After all, how could she? Her experience with men was non-existent.

'You don't know if you're sure?'

'No.' She bit into her lower lip again. 'I know… I know what I want.'

And she did. God help her, she did.

His smile then was her undoing. Slow to

spread and ever so sensual, it lit a thousand little fires beneath her skin.

'It's just…you're…you…'

His eyes flashed with something dark.

'Yes, and?' He moved closer to her, reaching for her strap and sliding it down a little way so he could press a kiss to the naked flesh of her shoulder. Thought and sense fled.

What had she been trying to say?

What did she want from him?

She knew this night would mean nothing to Adrastos. His reputation preceded him, and, besides that, Poppy had taken a vested interest in the string of broken hearts he left in his wake. To a man like Adrastos, sex was nothing. She'd even heard him say as much, to his father of all people, when King Alexander had challenged his heir about his overactive love life.

'Why shouldn't I enjoy myself before signing my life away to serve this country?'

That was what tonight was.

Enjoyment.

Pleasure.

If Poppy overthought it, she'd be the one backing out, and she knew she didn't want to do that.

'But nothing,' she said after a beat. Then thought better of it. 'No one can find out about this.' She couldn't imagine how she'd ever be able to explain this to Ellie, or his parents.

His eyes narrowed, raking over her face, his lips tweaked into a slight frown. 'I wasn't planning on publicising it.'

'No,' she said, wondering why his quick agreement didn't fill her with the rush of relief it should have. 'I don't know how I'd face your parents, or your sister…'

'It's no one else's business.'

'I know.' She swallowed. She should really tell him about her lack of experience…but what if he changed his mind? What if…?

It didn't matter. She wasn't tricking him into taking her virginity. She just knew he'd have thoughts about that, that he'd feel betrayed if she didn't give him any kind of warning or preparation.

'I have to tell you something,' she said, but as an insurance policy she took a page out of his book, reaching around to the zip at the back of her dress and sliding it down slowly, her skin lifting in goosebumps as she anticipated what was to come next.

'Go on.' He crossed his arms over his naked chest, but his eyes devoured her body, watching as the silky fabric slipped lower, and lower again, revealing a lace bra and matching panties.

'I'm going to tell you,' she said with a nod, more to herself than to him. 'But you need to promise me it won't change anything.'

'I promise.'

She rolled her eyes again. 'You don't even know what I'm going to say.'

'No, but I'm telling you, right now, you could say anything on earth and it wouldn't change what I want to happen.'

His certainty was its own aphrodisiac.

'I'm waiting.'

She nodded, nerves firing through her belly now.

'Poppy?'

He moved closer, his warmth enveloping her, as his hands came around to her bra and unclasped it with effortless ease, reminding her how often he did this kind of thing. His mouth on her nipple caught her completely off guard and she cried out, tilting her head back instinctively to provide better access. His tongue encircled her areola and she whimpered because the feeling was so exquisite and sensual, heat pooled inside her and warmth slicked between her legs.

'Adrastos…' she groaned, and thought was no longer possible.

'Can what you want to tell me wait until afterwards? Because, frankly, I need this like you wouldn't believe.' Not you. *This.* And to emphasise his point, he ground his arousal against her sex, so she felt the rock-hard heat of him and whimpered, moving her hips to be closer to him, needing so much of what he promised. He dragged his mouth to her lips at the same time he lifted her, cupping her bottom and holding her right against his arousal so if it weren't for the barrier of their remaining clothes, he could have sunk inside her, taking her and pleasuring her as she'd been dreaming about all these long years.

He pushed her back against the wall of the room, holding her there with his body, his mouth ravishing hers, his hands roaming her skin, feeling her, touching her, driving her crazy with his perfect, sublime nearness. But it wasn't enough. Maybe that was the point? She didn't have enough experience to know but she guessed this was a kind of foreplay—to make her want when she couldn't have, to fill her body with lust and desire until she was trembling and then take her just as she was about to lose her mind?

'Adrastos, please,' she cried out, her head hitting the wall as she tilted it back and stared at the ceiling, need bursting through her. In response, he repositioned himself so his arousal was pressed right against her sex, hard and strong even through his clothes, and he ground himself there as if they were actually together, so she was spinning out of control, pleasure making her eyes fill with stars.

'You are so sexy,' he said, and, even in her desire-addled state, she wondered why he sounded a little angry about that. 'So goddamned sexy.'

Sexy? And here Poppy had always thought herself lacking any kind of sex appeal whatsoever… 'I want you,' she said, simply, a sentence she'd thought many times in her head and never been able to speak aloud. Until now.

'Let's see about that,' he growled, catching her behind her bottom and carrying her once more, away from the wall and towards the bed, which he placed her in the middle of and brought his body over hers, staring down into her eyes. His hands found the elastic of her thong and slid it down her legs. He moved quickly and yet it was so sensual, his touch thorough and the air against her body cool. She shivered all over, earning a smile from Adrastos.

'Even better.' His eyes roamed her body with possessive heat, lingering on her breasts, her flat stomach, the apex of hair at the top of her thighs, admiration something she knew she wasn't imagining in his features.

Perhaps she should have expected it, given his last statement, and yet his touch against her sex was totally foreign to Poppy so she startled, jerking to a half-sitting position. His face shifted, focussing on her for a moment before he returned his attention to her womanhood, pressing a finger inside, and the totally unfamiliar sensation made her pulse riot and her body explode.

'Adrastos!' Now his name was a cry into the air, rent with passion. He moved his head upwards, pressing a sharp kiss against her lips, lingering there, his tongue striking hers.

'Shh,' he commanded into her mouth, with the hint of a laugh in the single sound. 'You are so loud, someone is bound to come and investigate.'

She wasn't sure she cared, in that moment. What mattered beyond this?

He pressed another finger into her, filling her so she arched her back and moaned, the pleasure so different, so full, so utterly indescribable.

'You are so wet,' he muttered and, for a moment, Poppy wondered if there was something wrong with that. She wished she had more experience, that she knew a little more about what they were doing and what Adrastos would want. 'So perfectly wet,' he said with a shake of his head. Not a bad thing, then.

He moved his mouth back to her breasts, flicking one then the other with his tongue as his fingers moved inside her, the rhythm in sync so she was facing multiple wildfires throughout her body, all of them burning out of control.

He drew his mouth lower, to her stomach, and then removed his hands from her breasts, pushing her legs apart and holding them wide, so she was momentarily bereft, because his touch was so perfect and she ached to feel him in her.

Only, he wasn't finished. The mouth that had driven her so wild by licking and sucking on her nipples pressed to her sex now, his tongue striking at her so she cried his name, pleasure saturating the syllables. She'd never imagined this could feel so…so…

'Oh, oh, oh…' she moaned as waves of pleasure built within her. His hands massaged her thighs and his tongue struck at her until she was crying out faster and faster, filling the room with the audible proof of her passion and then her release. She shook all over, trembling from head to toe as a new, terrifying and overpowering knowledge seeped into her body.

'Holy Mother of God,' she said with a shake of her head, breathing almost impossible, as he looked up at her, his expression one of utmost intensity. He stood with slow purpose, his hands unfastening his belt and removing it, placing it on the edge of the bed before he returned to his trousers, undoing the button first, then the zip. He moved at normal speed but to Poppy it was excruciatingly slow, because she wanted to feel, and she wanted to see. Sitting up when she was able, she wriggled to the edge of the bed and took over, her eyes hooked to his as she pushed his trousers down and then hooked her hands into the waistband of his briefs.

Desire exploded in her veins.

He was so beautiful. She was terrified of what was about to happen, but also absolutely sure it was what she wanted, no matter the consequences.

She pushed his underpants down, then realised she hadn't thought this through. His arousal was at her eye height and she had no idea what to do with that, only she felt she wanted things she didn't know enough about. She didn't want to disappoint him, and so, instead of leaning forward and taking him into her mouth, she lifted a hand to his shaft, wrapping her fingers around him and swallowing past a sudden lump in her throat. Because he was big. Not just big. Huge.

It startled her back to reality quicker than anything could.

He swore, the curse filling the room, and when she jerked her face to his, she saw that his eyes were closed, his skin pale, his lips compressed.

Had she done something wrong? She dropped her hand away quickly. 'You don't like to be touched?'

His eyes blinked open, fixing directly on her. 'Like it?' he repeated through clenched teeth. 'You think I didn't like that?'

'I... I'm not sure.'

He frowned slowly.

'Then let me be clear: I did. I do. But in the interest of honesty, if you touch me like that, I'm going to come, so don't do it again.'

She trembled, an unknown, unfamiliar power moving through her.

'Because I want *you*.'

More power, more pleasure, but also the shifting of certainty, doubts returning, and, thankfully, a hint of sanity. Urgency. She had to tell him that she'd never done this before.

'I want that as well,' she said after a pause, and, despite his warning, she lifted a hand to his base and wrapped her fingers around him, smiling at the sound of air hissing between his teeth.

'Poppy.' Her name held a warning.

'Adrastos,' she replied in kind, growing bold, moving her hand up and down his length, smiling at his ragged breath and the bead of liquid that pearled his tip. She might have been a twenty-four-year-old virgin, but instincts were stronger than experience, it turned out. Curiosity had her leaning forward, her heart racing with nerves as she pressed her lips to his arousal and tasted his essence, groaning as it hit her mouth.

He swore again, and this time pulled away from her, out of her reach, hands on hips, dark eyes glittering with emotions she didn't understand.

'That's enough.'

She was being pulled from one direction to the next. Had she done something wrong?

Or was it that he'd enjoyed it too much?

She wished she understood.

'That's enough,' he growled, moving back to the bed and quickly coming down over her. He was rough, she was smooth. He was hard, she was soft. His chest hairs brushed against her breasts, and the tip of his arousal, which she'd just taken into her mouth, was now at the entrance to her womanhood. They were seconds away from something she'd always wanted. Something she wanted with *him*, and no one else.

But she had no idea what it would be like for him, what he'd think if he realised she was a virgin. Despite the fact she wanted him with the power of a thousand suns, she wasn't going to risk breaching a moral wall she suspected he would value.

'I need to tell you something *now*, Adrastos.'

He made another noise, a hiss, as he pushed on his elbows and stared down at her, eyes piercing her, face flushed, lips parted.

But he waited, hitched at her sex, body held perfectly immovable.

Nerves flooded her, and desire was making it hard to think straight—harder still to do what she knew she needed to.

'I'm—'

'Damn it, Poppy, are you sure this conversation cannot wait until afterwards?'

Maybe this wasn't really a big deal. Maybe he wouldn't notice. Maybe, maybe, maybe…

'Poppy?'

He was right there, and it felt so good, so natural, so right, she simply nodded, surrendered, gave herself to what was about to happen and hoped for the best. What else could she do?

But she was didn't want him to stop and when he thrust into her, it was as though her whole body were exploding with bright white light. Pain at first, searing, sharp, overpowering, so she stilled, eyes wide, locked to his, lips pale from how hard she was compressing them, and her own sensations were so strong that she almost didn't see the expression on his face, almost didn't read the shock and incredulity in his eyes.

But then, pain receded as quickly as it had come, leaving a new sort of awareness, of being full of someone else, of having him so deep inside her, of being pleasured from the inside out.

'Poppy.' His voice was strangled, deep, a warning in the depths of his tone, but a warning to whom and about what?

'Please,' she said again, arching her hips instinctively, so he groaned, his own expression held tight now, his eyes pushing into hers and the rest of him completely still. 'Please,' she repeated, knowing she wanted this desperately.

He swore then, dipping his head forward, shielding his face from hers. Was it over? Was he going to end this? Then, he moved, pulling halfway out of her and pushing back in, rolling his hips, lifting his face to watch her, studying her, reading her and seeing what brought her pleasure, what she responded to, so Poppy closed her eyes and drifted away on a growing wave of sensuality.

Adrastos had never had a problem with stamina before. He prided himself on being able to pleasure a woman multiple times before finally succumbing to his own release, but Poppy was so tight, and her inexperience made her responses so completely innate. It wasn't just that she felt good, it was that she was in awe of how good she felt, shocked by her body's ability to respond to a man. Her eyes were wide, her skin dewy with sweat, her body trembling all over. It was the single most incredible experience of his life even when, in the back of his mind, an anger was building that he couldn't fathom nor explain.

Only he knew every reservation he'd had about this, every fibre of conscience, had been right. Poppy was not like the women he usually took to bed. Not only was she considered a part of his family, she had, until a moment ago, been a goddamned virgin.

Anger charged through him, taking over his need for release, so even as he moved inside Poppy and watched her fall apart for perhaps the first time in her life, he knew he would not succumb to his own yearning, aching need to finish.

He waited for her cries to soften, for her breathing to come back to normal, for her muscles to stop convulsing around him, and when she blinked up at him with eyes that were slightly sheened with tears, he felt an ocean of regret build inside his chest.

A lack of confidence had never been Adrastos's problem, and yet…living your life in someone else's shoes, as he'd been forced to, meant you second-guessed yourself a lot. The comparisons were inevitable. How Nicholas had been, how he'd lived, what he would have been like if he'd still been here today. One thing was for sure: he would never have given into temptation with a woman his parents viewed as a daughter. This was his *family*, for God's sake, and his family had already been through enough.

Adrastos pulled out of her quickly, as though he'd been burned, the faint smear of colour on his still rock-hard arousal all the evidence he needed that what he'd felt had indeed been the physical barrier of her innocence.

Silence sparked in the room, charged with his fury, so the air seemed to almost dance with electricity. Poppy lay there, her breasts shifting as she struggled to properly regain her breath, as she made sense of the feelings that were wracking her inexperienced body, so Adrastos had to turn away from her, to do his best to control his own breathing, to will his arousal into submission, and, most importantly, to stop himself from saying something he'd regret.

Because while he was angry at Poppy, it would be wrong to take that anger out on her in this moment. Whatever else this night had been, it was her birthday, and he'd unwittingly become her first lover.

He groaned, the magnitude of that inescapable. The kiss had been bad enough! But this bound them in a way, and always would. What the hell had he done? Panic was a surging tide, threatening to drown him. Adrastos wanted to shout into the room, to issue a denial, to take it all back. He would *never* be bound to anyone, especially not Poppy. It was the one small beacon of independence he held. His life, his right to date whom he wanted, his sexual freedom. Having sex with a virgin carried more meaning than the simple act of two people coming together—and knowing he'd been Poppy's first? What had he done? What had she let him do?

'Adrastos?' Her voice was soft and sweet, tremulous. 'Look at me.'

He closed his eyes hard, so little cracks formed at the edges of his face, then turned, his expression now stiff, his face bearing a mask of cool indifference even when inside he was a torrent of feelings. 'You were a virgin.'

He didn't need her to confirm it, but it felt somehow important to speak those words aloud.

Her eyes darted around the room and then she nodded, once. Her cheeks were stained pink.

'You're twenty-four.'

'I know that,' she whispered, not meeting his eyes.

He tried to control his anger. After all, it wasn't directed at Poppy—not all of it, anyway. Virgin or not, he shouldn't have brought her here, shouldn't have agreed to kiss her and 'not stop'.

'Why did you proposition me?' he demanded, remembering belatedly that she'd instigated this. He'd had no idea of her inexperience, but Poppy had known. And she'd goaded him into being her first!

'I—just—'

'You just what?' His words cracked around the room, frustration evident in the resounding bite of his syllables.

'I just wanted—'

'Sex? To lose your virginity?' he accused,

jacking his thumb towards the wall behind her. 'Well, there are about two dozen men out there who would have happily obliged. Why the hell did you choose me?'

'It wasn't— I just wanted—'

The night Nicholas had died, Adrastos had felt terrifyingly out of control, and he'd hated it. His world had crumbled and Adrastos hadn't held any power to stop that, to change it. Afterwards, he'd done everything he could to retain a grip on his life. He never let himself feel more than he wanted, never lost himself in sentiment or emotion, except for two times in his adult life: in the rose garden on Poppy's twenty-first birthday, and now. Even with his family, he'd pulled back just enough to protect himself from any more loss.

He'd worked hard to call the shots in every aspect of his life. But he hadn't been in control from the moment Poppy had approached him at the party, and that sense of powerlessness was bringing back subconscious echoes of how he'd felt when Nicholas had died, making him react stronger, harder, out of a fierce need for self-preservation.

'It's not a big deal, is it?'

The soft question had his head pounding as if it might explode. He jerked away from her, needing space to cool down, reaching for his boxer shorts and dragging them on his body. Her flimsy underwear lay at his feet and he scooped the thong up swiftly and tossed it in the direction of the bed.

'Get dressed.' The words were curt, and he had his back turned to her—more self-preservation—so didn't see the way her face paled and lower lip trembled.

'Why won't you look at me?' she whispered, a moment later, and so he had to steel himself to do exactly that, turning as he roughly buttoned up his shirt, then wishing he hadn't when the sight of her made Adrastos feel as though he'd been punched right in the middle of his chest.

She was dressed in her bra and pants, but her hair was tumbled and loose and her lips bruised from his kisses, her body so beautiful and fragile. His damned arousal jerked and he wanted to run. To literally run a marathon, to get this frantic, desperate energy out of his system.

He tried to regain control, to be reasonable, to take the edge off his anger, but he felt powerless and used. Yes, he felt used. She'd wanted to lose her virginity, she'd chosen him, to hell with the consequences. To hell with how that could potentially have affected his family.

'This was a mistake,' he said firmly. 'You are like a daughter to my parents, a sister to my sister.'

She tilted her chin with unexpected defiance. 'But not a sister to you.'

He felt nauseous. 'God, Poppy. You *should* be like a sister to me. After your parents died, my parents all but adopted you. You are their goddaughter. They raised you since you were fourteen.'

She closed her eyes. 'Thank you for the biographical information but I'm aware of all that already.'

He ground his teeth. 'This isn't the time for sarcasm.'

'I'm sorry, I've never done this before. How should I be acting?'

'Apologetically,' he muttered.

'You want me to apologise?'

'You know this shouldn't have happened.'

'You came in here very willingly…'

His eyes flashed with frustration. 'I had no idea you were a virgin. How the hell could I have known? You're twenty-four!'

'Yeah, well, we don't all live the way you live, Your Highness,' she snapped.

Her attitude was only making his anger worse. He didn't want to be reminded of his lifestyle in that moment. Strangely, it felt inappropriate to bring the shadow of other women into this room, now. 'Fine, but surely you've had boyfriends?'

The pink in her cheeks deepened.

'Poppy? You've had boyfriends, haven't you?' But Adrastos already knew the answer to that. He frowned, staring at her without seeing, as he realised the truth. Not once had a man been mentioned in connection to Poppy. He'd met a few of Eleanor's boyfriends, but never had Poppy brought someone home. Not once had her mother called him excitedly about some guy Poppy was dating, as she had for some of Ellie's men.

'So what?' she muttered, and something in the region of his heart splintered, something sharp and painful. Suddenly, Poppy was fourteen again, her cheeks tear-stained as she sat sobbing in the library, when he'd known he'd move heaven and earth to stop Poppy from ever feeling like that again, when he'd felt some strange sense of imperative to remove that pain from her life. They shared that grief—Poppy was better at expressing it, but it was inside Adrastos too, growing as a tree, wild and out of control at times.

'You should have told me,' he finished, his anger evaporating on a wave, leaving only a sense of sick disappointment in himself, and a sense that this was all going to get much worse.

'I meant to.'

He closed his eyes, remembering her insistence that she wanted to tell him something and the way it hadn't seemed anywhere near as important as losing himself in her.

He swore then, a short curse filling the air like an explosion. ‘You should have just said it. I deserved to know.’

‘And you’d have stopped.’

Anger whipped again. ‘Excuse me?’

‘You would have stopped what we were doing.’

‘So you *chose* not to tell me, to trick me, into being your first?’

She blanched. Perhaps she hadn’t consciously realised what she was doing, but that was what it amounted to.

‘You had no right.’ He pushed home his point. ‘Of course I would have stopped. That would have been the right thing to do. Damn it, Poppy. This was—a mistake.’

‘I don’t want you to feel that,’ she said quietly. ‘I—I don’t want to be something you regret.’

‘It’s a little late for that.’

He glared at her and now, fully dressed, if somewhat dishevelled-looking, he stalked to the internal door of the room, wrenched it open and strode out, slamming it behind him with a dull thud.

He had to get the hell away from her, to go for that run, to hope like hell he could push this from his mind. The one saving grace was that nobody knew what they’d done.

CHAPTER THREE

'OH, CRAP... OH, CRAP.' She pushed her mahogany-brown hair back from her eyes and blinked several times to focus on the screen of her phone as words swam before her over-tired eyes.

The taste of champagne rose in her throat and Poppy winced as she remembered how many glasses she'd consumed in rapid succession after rejoining the party, in an attempt to blot out the events that had transpired.

She stared at Ellie's text and prayed to any god who'd listen that somehow Poppy had misunderstood.

Please tell me nothing actually happened between you and Adrastos?

Memories sliced through Poppy and, despite the argument that had come after, all she felt was the rush of desire and awareness, of tingling, sensual heat as she felt again the sensations that had twisted inside her as Adrastos had kissed her, held her, touched her and finally made her his. Heat coloured Poppy's cheeks and slicked between her legs.

But why would Ellie even ask? Was it possible she'd said something after glass number however many of champagne?

She swiped out of the message and into another, this one from Ellie and Adrastos's mother—Poppy's godmother—Her Majesty Queen Clementine Aetos.

Darling? Call me when you get this. We need to talk.

Panic drummed through her. No one knew what had happened. No one. Unless Adrastos had said something?

To his parents? Not bloody likely. With a growing sense of trepidation and flashes of memories and experience garnered over years of living adjacent to the royal family, she thought of the microscope that was trained on Adrastos's life by a well-meaning but nonetheless outrageously invasive public. His every move was reported on, the tantalising speculation surrounding each of his brief, high-profile relationships something with which Poppy was all too familiar.

But this was different.

He hadn't taken Poppy to a movie premiere or dancing at a nightclub. Their dalliance was a secret, it had taken place behind closed doors and, afterwards, Poppy had gone back to the party and pretended nothing had happened. Adrastos had left by the time she'd emerged.

So what had happened in the eight or so hours since she'd come home and flopped into bed, and now?

With fingers that were shaking, she loaded a browser on her phone and typed first her name, then deleted it and typed Adrastos's instead.

And grimaced.

Sure enough, several of the trashier papers were already running the story, salivating at Poppy's connection to the royal family, so her heart was beating so hard in her chest it was like a heavy, metallic drum. Adrenalin filled her veins.

The first photo was benign enough—it showed Adrastos in the corridor outside the bedroom. While there was little scope to misinterpret what he'd just been doing—that he had dressed in haste was clear—it didn't necessarily implicate Poppy. And though she was hungry to understand the rest of the story, she couldn't help but idle on that image a moment, to stare at his face—thunderclouds would barely describe the emotion on his symmetrical features.

Swallowing, she quickly scrolled down and then saw the truly damaging image: a photo of Poppy on the balcony, cinched in against Adrastos and being kissed as though… She trembled. Was that really what it had been like? Just looking at the photo almost seared her with passion and urgency.

She dropped her phone like a hot potato.

'Darling Poppy…'

Clementine's voice was soft, and Poppy knew the Queen well enough to be able to perfectly picture the expression her face would bear.

'I find myself in a very difficult position.'

Poppy closed her eyes on the squirming sense of guilt. She had ignored several more calls from Eleanor and the royal courtiers but when the Queen herself began to ring, Poppy found it impossible not to answer. She didn't know what she'd say, but figured she would work it out as the conversation progressed. Only now, she was uncharacteristically lost for words.

'When your parents passed away, I was determined to bring you home with us. I was determined to raise you as my own, to love you as they did. I knew I could never replace your own dear mother, but I was desperate that you would know a mother's love, that you would know how adored and wanted you were.'

Tears filled Poppy's eyes.

'It is what I know your mother would have

done for my children, had we—had anything happened to us.'

Poppy bit down on her lower lip.

'You have been a part of our family for a long time and I am grateful every day for that.'

A lump formed in Poppy's throat. She felt lower than low.

'But that means you *know* us better than anyone else.'

Ice spread through Poppy. *Us.* It was one tiny word, one of the smallest in existence, but its weight was hefty, for it made Poppy instantly feel like an outsider. She grimaced, pressed her back against the wall and tried to breathe in and feel strong.

'Adrastos is a good man, and he will be an excellent king, but there can be no misunderstanding where his priorities are in his personal life.'

Clementine's voice, though still soft, was also heavy; it carried a sadness that Poppy had heard before, usually when some Adrastos scandal or other had landed him in the papers. It didn't matter though what Adrastos did in his personal life. He was so roguishly charming that even his pathological inability to commit was looked on with fondness by the public. Only within the palace did it cause serious, ground-shaking despair. And now Poppy was a part of that narrative.

'Your Majesty,' she said, reverting to Clementine's title. It felt appropriate, in the circumstances. Guilt was searing her. She knew what the family thought of Adrastos's philandering. Having slept with him somehow made Poppy complicit in that. She couldn't bear for them to think she didn't take their worries seriously, that she didn't *understand* why they held such concerns. 'I wish I knew what to say…'

Clementine sighed. 'He's gone too far this time. And at your birthday party. At *Ellie's* party!'

'The photos are misleading,' she murmured, trying to pull on all her legal training to connect the dots. What did the evidence show? What could be proven? But Poppy had never been a good liar, she'd never felt comfortable with any elimination of the truth, no matter how small, and lying to Clementine felt particularly wrong. And yet, the situation was so complicated. Wasn't it sometimes better to blur the lines, just a little, if doing so was harmless and the result eased another person's suffering? 'We thought we were alone.'

'You thought you were alone, but Adrastos should have known better,' Clementine huffed. 'He has lived this life long enough to know there are very few places where privacy is assured.'

Poppy's eyes narrowed. She conjured an image of Adrastos, seeing him as he was: strong, indomitable, a force of pure energy and courage, and imagined how little Clementine's criticism would upset someone like him. Only it wasn't fair. None of this was Adrastos's fault. He'd simply done exactly what she'd asked.

'Oh, Poppy.' Clementine sighed. 'I cannot help wondering how and why this happened. You *know* what he is like. The King is beside himself. The idea of Adrastos involving *you* in his lifestyle, the idea of him treating *you* like the others…'

Poppy made a chortled sound of disbelief. She had worried she might be exiled and, instead, the Queen was simply *worrying* about Poppy. Worrying because of Adrastos's reputation. Well, she wasn't wrong, and yet an unexpected protective instinct licked through her, and she thought of the time in the library, many years ago, when Adrastos had found Poppy crying and promised her that everything would be okay. She'd felt his protectiveness and his protection and those feelings moved through her again now, only it was Adrastos she wanted to protect and defend.

'It's not like that,' she mumbled, speaking almost without thinking. 'I promise, it's different.'

Clementine was so quiet, and that silence should have given Poppy time to think, to reflect on the words that were forming in her mouth, but all she could think about was how much she wanted to spare Adrastos from his parents' criticism. After all, she'd seduced Adrastos. The whole thing had been *her* idea. True, he'd gone along *very* willingly, but he wouldn't have touched her with a ten-foot bargepole if he'd known about her innocence—a point he'd made blindingly clear immediately afterwards.

Poppy winced.

'Generally, the palace doesn't comment on Adrastos's…business,' Clementine said with obvious distaste. 'But you are our goddaughter, and everyone knows it. Anders would like to discuss the best way forward, the best damage control, if you will.'

When Clementine referred to the King's private secretary, Poppy knew it was a really big deal. Anders didn't get involved in anything beneath his pay grade.

Suddenly, Poppy felt that she was in way over her head. It was all too much.

'I'm just so disappointed, Poppy, in both of you, if I'm honest. How can our family proceed after this?'

Poppy felt the world crumbling beneath her, she felt the reality she was facing. Clementine might have been angrier at Adrastos, she might have pitied Poppy her stupidity in having a one-night stand with him, but, when push came to shove, he was their son and heir to the throne and if things became awkward it was Poppy who'd face exile from the family, not Adrastos. She couldn't lose them! This family was all she had.

It was vital to find a way through this that spared the King and Queen from feeling awkwardness, from having to make the difficult decision to cut Poppy from their family's lives.

'He should have known you, of all people, were off limits, but he cannot help himself, it seems. I am so disappointed,' she repeated. 'And you know what he is like! You know better!'

Poppy flinched. None of this was meant to be in the public sphere. It had been her personal moment, a personal triumph. She'd lost her virginity and now the whole world knew about it. Not that she'd been innocent, but that she'd been taken to bed by the great philanderer Adrastos Aetos.

'You do know better, don't you, darling? I have tried to raise you as your mother would have, to instil sense and reason, to guide you. I wouldn't have thought...' The Queen trailed off, lost in thought, and Poppy cringed, feeling as though she'd badly let down her godmother.

Clementine sighed, rallied, began to speak once more, a different tack this time, no less effective. 'You've worked so hard, Poppy, but what about your professional credibility?' the Queen murmured. 'You were so eager to establish yourself all on your own, without our help and contacts, without any connection to us. Surely you can see how damaging this will be to your reputation?'

'It's not the nineteenth century,' Poppy couldn't help pointing out. 'My private life is still my own. I cannot see that it will have any impact on my work.'

'That's naïve,' Clementine said gently, with sad affection. 'And idealistic. Of course it *shouldn't* impact your work, but it will. Events like this have a habit of taking over, of becoming all that a person is known for. Your professional successes will be mentioned as an afterthought to this. You must have known how many ripples in the pond would come from spending the night with Adrastos?'

Poppy felt as though she might vomit, and it had nothing to do with all the champagne she'd drunk after sleeping with Adrastos. The picture Queen Clementine painted was suitably dire, and, unfortunately, not entirely inaccurate. Poppy was well respected in her role as a human rights lawyer but none of her achievements would ever be mentioned before this piece of gossip. There would be whispers behind her back for a long time to come now her night with Adrastos was public knowledge.

Unless…

She sat up straighter, stared at the wall, an idea

coming to her quite out of nowhere. It seemed crazy at first, but as she held the idea in the front of her mind and examined it from all angles, she realised it wasn't crazy so much as the only way through this that might preserve her professional reputation, save Adrastos from his parents' wrath, and also make it possible to maintain the status quo within the family—something that meant more to her than she could ever put into words.

'Your Majesty, there's something I have to tell you...'

Poppy moved with greater dexterity than she'd been capable of summoning half an hour earlier. She changed into a pair of jeans, a turtleneck skivvy and a faux fur jacket, dashed some bright lipstick into place and finger-combed her hair over one shoulder, before donning dark sunglasses and pulling open the front door of her house with one mission in mind: she had to speak to Adrastos.

But as soon as the door opened, she was blinded—by the startling winter sun first, then the flashes of a thousand cameras.

'Oh, my God.'

She dipped her head forward, pulling the door shut quickly and moving through the pack, numb and terrified at the same time. Why hadn't she anticipated this? Because she'd been a bundle of nerves and emotions since waking. Everything had happened so fast, like a snowball caught in an avalanche, and Poppy hadn't dared take time to stop and think about whether or not this course of action was wise: it was the only solution, so she'd had to pursue it.

'Poppy, is it true you're secretly engaged to the Prince?'

'Poppy, how do you feel about him? Is it love?'

'Poppy, Poppy, Poppy!'

She walked quickly, fingernails digging into her palms, but the photographers followed her as a swarm of bees might ambush a picnic, so she was regretting her decision to have this conversation face to face. Only she *had* to see Adrastos. She was a tumble of feelings and nerves, and while seeing him might make it worse, it would also, she thought with crossed fingers, make it somehow better.

Paparazzi engulfed her until she reached her car, parked on the narrow street of Stomland's capital that she'd called home ever since moving out of the palace to attend university. Her parents had left her an inheritance and on her eighteenth birthday it had matured, enabling her to buy the charming, historic townhouse in a little mews location. While the King and Queen hadn't wanted Poppy to move out, it had felt important to Poppy to repay their generosity with a sign of independence.

Or was it that, deep down, she'd been afraid to wear out her welcome?

They'd always made her feel like a part of the family, but she wasn't, not really, and that idea kept scrolling through her mind as she slipped into the driver's seat and started the engine.

Still the photographers snapped away and she couldn't help wondering why. Surely they had whatever image they would need by now?

With a look of exasperation, she pulled out from the kerb and began to drive to the home she knew Adrastos lived in, but had never personally been to, with a growing sense of trepidation and disbelief. Was she really going to ask him to do this?

When Nicholas had died, Adrastos had wanted, more than anything, to find a way to turn time backwards, to go back into the past and see Nicholas again, to be able firstly to fix him, and, failing that, to be able to *tell* him everything he felt, everything he thought. As boys, they'd been competitive: separated by only thirteen months, one the heir, the other a backup, they'd been pitted against each other without their realising it at first.

It didn't help that Adrastos had been bigger

and stronger. He'd walked from a younger age than Nicholas had, he'd run, jumped, talked younger. He'd been faster. More confident and charming, and, though he hadn't been consciously aware of it, Adrastos had enjoyed the competition, for he'd always won.

But when Nicholas had died, Adrastos had regretted having competed with him. He'd regretted taking every opportunity to show his superiority. He'd wanted to rewind his life and do it differently, better. A complex, heavy thought for a teenager to have, nonetheless, it had been clear as anything in Adrastos's mind.

And now, staring at the front page of the newspaper, he felt that same desperate, foolish longing. He wanted to go back in time and undo it all. What the hell had he been thinking?

She'd propositioned him, sure, but he was older, wiser, clearly more experienced. So why the hell hadn't he just flat out refused? Why had he gone outside with her? Breathed her in? Kissed her. Held her body against his?

He groaned, dropping his head forward with a sinking feeling in his gut.

Nobody dared question his lifestyle choices publicly. He was aware of his parents' feelings, aware of the headache it gave the courtiers who ran—or attempted to run—their lives, but no one had been brave, or stupid, enough to directly criticise him for his almost pathological need to enjoy a woman's company.

That, he suspected, was about to change. Poppy was no ordinary woman. There was no way his parents would let this infraction go without some dialogue.

And worse, what would it do to their family?

It was almost Christmas, a time of year when they came together and ate around the table *en famille*, Poppy included. Were they all to ignore the elephant in the room?

Not for the first time, he fantasised about not going, but even Adrastos couldn't do that. Not to his parents, who had buried their oldest child, who existed in a strange half-life, here in the present even as they were simply going through the motions, waiting to be joined with Nicholas again.

Adrastos grunted, stood, paced his living room then paused as a noise alerted him to something beyond his door.

The paparazzi scrum outside her own apartment was nothing compared to the assembly of photographers waiting at Adrastos's. However, at least there was a security presence here to keep them at bay. Adrastos had four military guards on his front steps, as well as a dozen security cameras set up on the façade of his beautiful residence. Poppy hadn't been able to park anywhere near his home, so she walked the last of the way, on the opposite side of the street until the last possible moment to avoid the attention of the paparazzi and then, with her head down, across the street and straight into the lion's den.

It was fortunate for Poppy that one of the security guards saw her first, putting an arm around her shoulders and leading her up the steps and to the front door before shepherding her inside swiftly, but not before the clicking of cameras had almost deafened her.

She looked around just as Adrastos stalked into the tiled, double-height foyer, and the logical, calm-sounding explanation she'd concocted on the drive across town burst into flames on the periphery of her mind as everything went blank except the sheer euphoria and electrical charge of seeing him again.

Her pulse went crazy, her mouth dry, her fingers began to tingle and her stomach twisted and tightened until she could hardly breathe.

'Adrastos.' His name was barely audible, a throaty, emotional noise from the depths of her gut.

'You shouldn't have come,' he grunted, evidently feeling none of the temptation at seeing Poppy again that she was managing being confronted by Adrastos.

She tried to control her nerves, to calm her rapidly firing pulse, but she was awash with sensation. It was about a thousand times worse than her first trial, when she'd had to stand up and argue in front of a judge.

'We have to talk.'

His jaw moved as though he were grinding his teeth. Contemplating rejecting her?

'It's important.'

'I have not changed my mind about last night, Poppy. It was a mistake. One of the worst of my life. Talking about it will not alter that.'

She flinched. Okay, she hadn't expected him to be jumping for joy about it all, but to refer to it in such bald terms made something in the region of her heart ache unbearably.

'I don't want to talk about last night,' she answered after a brief, painful pause.

His brows lifted. 'I cannot imagine we have anything else to discuss.'

Poppy rolled her eyes, an expression that he evidently hadn't expected, because his gaze narrowed and surprise briefly flitted in the depths of his pupils. 'You know that's not true.'

Perhaps he did, because a moment later, with a look of resignation, he gestured towards the doorway that led from the foyer into what appeared to be a living area.

'Fine. Let's talk, then.'

But he didn't move, and in order to step in the direction he'd gestured, Poppy had to therefore walk past Adrastos, and even passing within two inches of his tall, masculine frame had her pulse skittering wildly, memories slamming into her so she gasped and quickly looked away, digging her nails into her palms and willing her brain to engage, to take over, so other parts of her body didn't start calling the shots.

I want you to kiss me, and this time, I want you to not stop.

Had she really said that to him? She was in awe of her bravery, and stupidity. All of this was her fault. And now she'd gone and made it all so much worse…by doing the only thing she could think of that would ultimately fix it.

Poppy had come here to talk, but, having never been in Adrastos's house, she couldn't help the curiosity that flooded her as she stepped into his living room and looked around. The décor was similar to the palace, only a little less intricate, more modern. There was a distinct lack of personal touches—no photographs or artwork on the walls, no candles or flowers. It was like a five-star hotel, she thought with a small frown, the kind of place one could walk into and out of without a thought.

'Have you spoken to anyone today?' She turned slowly to face him, her mouth parched once more as he rolled up the buttoned shirt sleeves to reveal tanned, toned forearms.

'I have,' he said with a dip of his head. 'The prime minister, about a trade deal with Argentina, my valet too.'

She fought the urge to roll her eyes again. 'I mean about last night.' Then, with an embarrassed whisper, 'About us.'

'No, Poppy,' he drawled. 'That has not been on the top of my priority list.'

'Your mother hasn't called you?'

He frowned. 'Not yet.'

'She will,' Poppy muttered.

'I take it she has called you?'

'Her, Eleanor, Anders,' she said, tapping her fingers to enumerate the list as she mentioned each name. 'I'm surprised the King himself didn't beat a path to my door to find out what the heck we were thinking.'

'I would struggle to give an explanation to that question,' he said grimly.

'Me too.' She pressed her teeth into her lower lip. 'But we did sleep together, and there are photos that make it pretty obvious. We can't change what happened, so we have to manage the consequences.'

'Consequences?' His brows shot up and he stared at her with pale skin, a look on his face that Poppy didn't understand. He swore then, moved closer, wrapped one hand around her forearm. 'You're not telling me you're pregnant?'

Poppy's heart did a funny little skip and she immediately envisaged the children they could have—their children—and an emptiness opened up in the centre of her being. A real family. Her own family. She quickly shook her head. 'Surely you know it's way too soon for that?'

'Of course,' he muttered, closing his eyes. 'I am not an idiot. And yet last night, I acted like one, well and truly. I cannot believe I was so stupid, so ignorant.'

She lifted a finger and pressed it to his lips. 'I'm on the pill,' she said gently, shocked to realise she almost wished that weren't the case. 'I have been for years.'

'But you're not sexually active.'

She didn't correct the tense he'd used. 'That's not the only reason people go on contraception,' she said with a lift of her shoulders. 'You can rest assured, the chances of me having conceived your baby are very, very slim.'

'But not impossible.'

She wrinkled her nose. 'Well, no, but very unlikely.'

His Adam's apple jerked as he swallowed. 'Is this what you wanted to discuss?'

'No. Until you mentioned it, the idea of a pregnancy hadn't even occurred to me.'

'Then what can I do for you, Poppy?'

He stepped backwards, withdrawing from her, removing himself incrementally until he was unfamiliar and strange, cold and detached.

She furrowed her brow. 'Don't be mad.'

He didn't visibly react, but she felt a shock wave move from him to her. 'About?'

Poppy wrung her hands in front of her chest. 'So I spoke to your mother this morning, and let's just say she was beside herself. She was angry at you, disappointed with me, worried for both of us, and she raised some very valid points about my career. You know how grateful I am to your family, how much I hate the idea of hurting them…'

His nostrils flared. 'What you and I do privately is of no concern to them, or anyone.'

'Do you really believe that?'

His eyes held hers for a long time and Poppy's concentration was failing, everything was fading, the world beyond them, the physical items in his home, even the air grew thin, as she felt only the insane connection between herself and Adrastos and an almost magnetic desire to act on it.

'I believe it's how it should be,' he conceded after a beat.

'So do I. But unfortunately, reality is different. We made a mess, Adrastos, and we have to clean it up.'

'And you have some brilliant idea for how to do this?'

'Well, I don't know if it's brilliant,' she said with a lift of her shoulders. 'In fact, on the drive over here, I kept thinking how *stupid* it is, but, getting to the point: I've already told your mother, the die is cast, and there's nothing for it but to carry on now.'

'You've told my mother what, exactly?'

Poppy sucked in a deep breath, tasting him on the tip of her tongue, wanting him, needing him. 'She hated the idea of me being just another one of your women,' she said, not noticing the way he stiffened. 'And I hated the idea of her thinking that too. So I told her… I told her…' Poppy groaned, then tilted her head back, staring up at the ceiling.

'You told her what?' he repeated, but with more urgency.

'That we're secretly dating,' she whispered. And then she waited for Adrastos to react.

CHAPTER FOUR

LIKE THE EYE of an epic storm, seconds passed in silence, and yet there was an undercurrent of pulsing, of raw, untameable energy, and then, Adrastos spoke, his voice controlled, but the kind of control that somehow sent Poppy's nerves into a state of abandon.

'You did what?'

'Hear me out,' she said, closing her eyes because it was impossible to look at him and see rejection on his face. She felt as though she'd dug an incredibly deep hole and he was the only person who could help her out of it. Until that moment, it hadn't really occurred to Poppy that he might not agree to. 'You must know how your parents feel about your, erm...'

She forced herself to blink in his general vicinity then, an unspoken plea on her face.

But Adrastos didn't help her out. He stood like a totem pole, massive and unyielding, arms crossed over his broad chest, eyes boring into her.

'Lifestyle,' she finished after a beat. 'Your

habits with women are well documented. They hate it, but they know better than to try to convey that to you, for fear you'll resent their interference so much you'll increase your, erm… activities.'

He barely reacted, but in his jaw, a muscle flexed.

'You are the heir to the throne. They want you to settle down.'

'You do not need to interpret my parents' feelings for me, Poppy. Whether they have expressed their wishes to me is beside the point: obviously they would rather I was married by now, with the obligatory minimum of two children.'

She pushed aside the strange, barbed feeling tightening at her chest.

'Sleeping with me was…' She hesitated. 'Well, they're annoyed.'

'So?'

She flinched. 'You might feel that way, but I sure as heck don't. I love your parents and the last thing I want to do is repay their generosity and kindness by disrespecting them, by disappointing them.' Her voice crackled with feeling.

'Again, Poppy, what you and I do in our personal lives…'

'That's not true. They're a part of my personal life. Eleanor is my *best friend.* Sleeping with you was…' But she couldn't say it was a mistake.

She couldn't say she regretted it. 'I wish no one had found out, but they did, and the only thing we can do to fix this is pretend it wasn't just a meaningless one-night stand,' she mumbled. 'A one-night stand *is* disrespectful. But a secret relationship?'

'I do not get involved in relationships. My parents know this better than anyone.'

'This isn't a real relationship,' she pointed out caustically, rubbing her fingertips to her temple, pushing aside the question she had. *Why didn't he get involved in relationships?* 'We'll pretend we're dating, that we like each other, but that we're taking it slowly because of the family situation. Can't you see that it makes everything better? Jeopardising my relationship with your family for a one-night stand is stupid and unthinking, but for a relationship…'

'Why did you do it, then?' he pushed. 'You knew all this last night,' he pointed out.

'I also told you expressly that no one could find out.'

He rocked back on his heels a little. 'That's hard to control, when you choose to sleep with someone like me.'

'I see that now.'

He sighed heavily. 'I'm sorry, Poppy, but I have no interest in pretending to date you.'

Her stomach dropped to her toes. 'Well, then,

you'll have to call your mother and tell her the truth,' Poppy said with a lift of her shoulders. 'Tell her your oversized libido couldn't pass up the opportunity to take my virginity,' she added with an extra shrug.

He glared at her. 'You are well aware I had no knowledge of that.'

'It doesn't change anything.'

He opened his mouth then closed it, rubbed a hand across his jaw. 'Have you thought about the timing of this? It's Christmas. We're about to spend almost two weeks at the palace, as we do every year.'

'I've thought of nothing else.' She groaned. 'But can't you see how much less awkward this will be, for everyone?'

His eyes were mocking. 'Really? You don't think there is an inherent awkwardness to us carrying on a faux relationship under my parents' watchful gaze? As for my sister, she will want all the details. Are you really prepared to lie to them?'

She shook her head and, to her chagrin, tears moistened her eyes. 'No. Yes. I hate the idea, of course. I hate it. But my back was against a wall,' she said honestly, before remembering the truth of that sentence, the way he had held her with her back against the wall, grinding his arousal into her.

But they both pictured that moment, she knew it. The air between them seemed to spark.

'Your mother was so…disappointed. I had to tell her something.'

'And what next, Poppy? Do we get fake engaged? Fake married?'

'No,' she almost shouted. 'God, no. We'll break up.' Poppy drew a deep breath. 'I've accepted a promotion, Adrastos, at The Hague. It's a huge opportunity for me. I leave early January.'

She waited for him to respond, but all he did was narrow his gaze slightly. Poppy swallowed. 'When the dust has settled on all this, we'll explain that I'm leaving, and given the geographical difficulties of a long distance relationship, we've decided we're better as…friends.' She faltered, because she hadn't thought of him as a friend for a very long time, probably not ever. 'They'll be a little disappointed, but not compared to how they'd feel if you immediately go back to sleeping with anything with a pulse.'

'You've really thought it all out, haven't you?'

'Not really,' she said with a humourless laugh. 'I acted without thinking it through at all, but I believe my instincts are right. This is the only way to save them from embarrassment, to avoid a ridiculous amount of scandal, and to save face in front of them. Don't you agree?'

He stared at her for a long time, and Poppy

found it impossible to know what he was thinking. But finally, he took two steps towards her, hands on hips, eyes now challenging rather than mocking.

'You are asking me to do this, for you,' he said quietly.

'For your parents—'

He shook his head. 'I am used to what my parents think of me. I would not be doing this to change that. But I understand why *you* need us to do this.'

She bit down on her lip, hating that a single tear fell from her eyes, hating that he saw her vulnerabilities as clearly as if they were writ across her breasts.

'So you agree?'

'Perhaps.'

A feeling like hope fluttered in her chest, but there was something else, too. A rush of adrenalin. A charge of fear. 'Perhaps?'

'You should be sure about what you are asking of me.' He moved a step closer, then surprised Poppy by reaching out and pressing his fingers to her chin, tilting her face so their eyes met squarely. 'You should be clear about what I would expect in return.'

Poppy's pulse went crazy. She couldn't speak for several moments and when she finally did, the words were trembly and weak.

'What would you expect?'

His smile was more of a smirk: damn him for even making that look sexy!

'My parents will only believe this if we are convincing. I would not agree to pretend to date you and then have them discover it was a lie. If we do it, it must seem real.'

'Obviously,' she snapped.

'At the palace, you will sleep in my room. In my bed.'

Her lips parted on a rush of surprise. 'I—can't see that that's necessary.'

Another smirk. 'You are so quick to point out that my parents know what I'm like. Do you really think they'd believe anything less?'

He had a very valid point. Damn it, why hadn't Poppy thought of that?

'But we can't—I'm not—suggesting we, erm—'

Nearer he came, closing the distance between them completely. 'Sleep together again?' he murmured, the words warm against her cheek.

'Right,' she said, uneasily, because her pulse was now just a tsunami in her veins and her knees were trembling.

'I cannot promise you that,' he said quietly.

She shivered, adrenalin making her body shake. 'You said it was a mistake,' she reminded him, shaking her head. Even when she desperately, desperately yearned for him, on some instinctive level, she knew that to give into that desire would be an absolute nightmare.

'Some mistakes are pleasurable to repeat.' And he kissed her, with as much intensity as their first kiss, more perhaps, because so much had happened since then, and her whole body responded with an arc of fierce, bright electricity and a burst of something like light that came from the depths of her soul and flared outwards. She wanted to cry and laugh and scream and melt into a puddle of pleasure at his feet, but all she could do was kiss him back, and wrap her hands around his neck and hold him closer to her, lift her body, press it against him, her breasts squashed to his chest, her hips so close to his manhood, her mind wishing away their clothes so that they could rediscover what they'd shared last night.

His tongue moved with devastating effect, rolling hers, teasing, his mouth punishing and proclaiming her as his even before she could understand what he was doing. She was exploding from every pore of her body; she was awash with sensations and then, into his mouth, she was begging for him. She didn't care. She needed him. It made no sense, but nothing about this did. Just like last night, she was overpowered by something so much bigger than her; she just hoped Adrastos could help her make sense of it all.

He pulled away and she stared up at him, bewildered, still flooded with an electrical current, body jolting, waiting for his hands to lift her shirt, to remove her clothes then his—but he stepped away from her instead, and his features bore a mask of cool reserve.

'There is no sense pretending you do not want to sleep with me, Poppy. We both know that is a lie.'

She gasped. Had he kissed her just to prove a point? God, and she'd let him. She'd let her objections go so quickly and easily.

She was trembling from anger now, and yes, desire too. 'Are you saying you'll only do this if I agree to…have sex with you?'

To his credit, he blanched. 'Do you honestly think I am desperate enough to deliver such an ultimatum?'

It wasn't the time to be reminded of his prowess with women.

'So?' she said crossly. 'What, then?'

'You will sleep in my bed. This is not negotiable. I will not agree to lie to my parents and then have that lie found out. We all have our boundaries: that is mine.'

She had to respect his position on that, particularly as she'd forced him into the lie.

'But you should realise that sex is a very real possibility of the situation you've orchestrated. If you have an issue with that, you should work out a way to extricate yourself now. Otherwise…' his eyes met hers, held, and a shiver ran the length of her spine '… I suggest you sit back and enjoy the ride.'

While Adrastos had earned a reputation as a playboy prince, he was also revered and respected for both his work ethic and nous, and with good reason. At nineteen, he'd been catapulted into the position of heir to the throne but his interest in good governance and social policies predated it. From almost as soon as he could remember, Adrastos had been fascinated by the way things worked, and, more importantly, by how he could make them better.

His position of authority simply gave him a vehicle for change, and he was not slow in using it.

However, as he pored over a report he would usually have devoured in a single hour, he found his concentration wandering, his focus bizarrely absent.

Or perhaps it wasn't so bizarre, he thought, leaning back in his broad leather chair and rubbing his palm over the back of his neck.

After all, the experience of making love to Poppy was still fresh in his mind, and though he'd done an admirable job of acting in control earlier that day, when she'd come to his home, Adrastos had kept a grip of his own desire with a maximum of effort.

When that tear had rolled down her cheek, he'd felt the same instincts that had overcome him as a teenager, when she'd arrived heartbroken and grief-stricken. He'd wanted to fix everything for her because he'd hated to see her in pain. He'd told himself it was because he knew loss and wished someone had been able to make it better for him, but now, he wasn't so sure. Maybe it was just… Poppy? Maybe there was something about her that inspired that protective streak?

He expelled a frustrated sigh, because it went way beyond wanting to protect her.

Last night had been about pure need, plain and simple.

But Poppy?

Sure, he'd wanted her. That was impossible to deny. But he could have had just about any single woman at that party—that wasn't arrogance speaking, so much as experience. And any woman would have been less complicated than this. Instead, her breathless little entreaty for him to kiss her and not stop had weaved through him, rebuilt him as a new man, a man who wanted, more than anything, to be with Poppy. He'd known she was forbidden. Hell, he'd had three years to regret that one damned kiss, to be thankful as anything he hadn't allowed it to go further. That should have been the salient lesson, the reminder that stopped him from acting on his desire.

Instead, he'd let one part of his anatomy do the talking.

Since Nicholas's death, Adrastos had had to walk in his brother's shadow—even when the papers feted and adored Adrastos and made comparisons praising him without, perhaps, realising that there was implied insult to Nicholas in those lines of adulation. Adrastos hated it. He had been happy enough to compete with Nicholas in life, but now, it wasn't fair, it wasn't right.

And yet he'd stepped up, taken on Nicholas's role, borne the survivor guilt that plagued him constantly, become what was expected of him, except in this one small regard: he was not going to be the dutiful heir and marry some available princess hand-selected for him by a royal courtier. He was not going to roll over completely and fall into line with what everyone wanted.

At first, sleeping with women, flirting with them, seducing them, had been a way to forget about Nick. To forget about love and loss and the powerlessness of an individual when faced with terminal illness. After Nicholas died, Adrastos had felt bad, all the time, except when he had sex. It was, therefore, an easy equation.

But then, he began to crave the criticism and disapproval, even when it was only something he glimpsed in his parents' faces, even when they tried so damned hard not to say what they were thinking.

He relished failing them, because he knew Nick never would have.

Nick would have married years ago. Someone appropriate and suitable. It was a small, stupid way to honour his brother's memory, to allow his brother to 'win' in their unspoken competition, but it was nonetheless important to Adrastos.

And now he'd unwittingly found himself in a relationship, albeit a pretend one, with the kind of woman his parents would be desperate for him to marry. He groaned audibly. Their break-up would be the ultimate disappointment, which should have satisfied him on some level. But he didn't feel satisfied. He didn't feel anything except numb.

He was regretting his acquiescence; he was regretting everything, but Adrastos was a man of his word, and he'd given that word to Poppy.

He'd made his bed, and now he had to lie in it. He wouldn't be alone though. Poppy had made sure of that. No wonder he couldn't focus on the report in front of him.

* * *

'I just can't believe this. How did it happen?'

Poppy grimaced. Lying to her best friend was the absolute worst, but it was a necessary evil. She'd looked at this from a thousand different angles before calling Eleanor, trying to see if there was any other way, if she could back out of the fib she'd unthinkingly told the Queen, but there was no solution at hand. If Eleanor, of all people, knew the truth, she'd be livid—at both of them. Poppy couldn't bear to let Ellie down.

'We just got talking one afternoon…'

'But you know what he's like, Pops.' Ellie groaned. 'You *know*.'

'People change,' she said, but she was cold to the centre of her being.

'You're really dating him?'

'We're getting to know each other. It's not serious—'

'But you're spending Christmas together.'

'Well…' Poppy bit into her lip until it hurt. 'I always spend Christmas with you.'

'And so does Adrastos, but this is different.'

Poppy felt lower than low. Yet, how could she tell Ellie the truth? Who knew how the Princess would react to the news that, instead of being in a relationship with Adrastos, Poppy had actually just lost her virginity to him in a super-sexy one-night stand? Hardly the kind of news a best friend would want to hear.

'Do you mind?'

The silence that followed Poppy's question was the longest of her life.

'It's weird,' Ellie admitted after a minute. 'You're my best friend and he's my brother. The thought of the two of you is hard to get used to. But it's more than that, Pops.'

Poppy waited, nerves stretching.

'I love Adrastos. It's just…he's different to you. He's…'

'More experienced,' Poppy said.

'I don't want you to get hurt,' Ellie urged.

'I promise you, I won't.'

There was no scope for her to be hurt because this wasn't a real relationship. He was faking it and so was she, more or less.

'Maybe he'll be different with you,' Ellie said, but her own voice showed ambivalence. 'Just… be careful. He's a great guy, but I've never seen him with a woman he hasn't treated as expendable. And you're most definitely not that.'

'We're taking it slow. I promise.'

Poppy disconnected the call with a tremor of anxiety. Taking it slow? Hardly. They were going to be sharing a room in the palace, doing their level best to convince his parents they were madly in love. This could be a recipe for disaster.

* * *

After her parents' deaths, this palace had become a salvation to Poppy. It was a place where she was loved and safe and, for four years of her life, it had been her home, day in, day out. Despite that, a kaleidoscope of butterflies took over her tummy as she went through the gates now—because for the first time, she was in the same car as Adrastos, their arrival carefully planned to ring with truth.

The act they'd discussed almost academically was about to begin and Poppy knew she had to give the performance of a lifetime.

With Adrastos.

Pretending that he was her lover!

Just the idea of that made her pulse race and her stomach twist. How could she possibly convince the people who knew her best?

But how could she not? Ever since those photos had run in the papers, more and more stories had been printed, each more fanciful than the next, the speculation quite wild, the interviews incredibly invasive. Because Poppy had refused to hold any media events herself—naturally—there'd been interviews with whomever the less scrupulous tabloids could drench up, from old school 'friends', to lecturers at university, never mind if Poppy had never been in their class. But with each article to run, Poppy became gladder they'd agreed to do this, to give some flesh to the fact they'd slept together. His family would be disappointed when they broke up, but at least they wouldn't think that either Poppy or Adrastos had been so stupid as to fall into bed together, to hell with how that would impact anyone else.

'Ready?' His voice was deep and gruff and made her already oversensitive nerves tremble. She turned to him slowly, her pulse all over the place, her heart twisting painfully. Their eyes met and she was tumbling through the cotton candy of her memories, straight back to that night, when he'd pulled her against him and kissed her until she saw stars.

'Adrastos?' Her eyes were huge, her skin pale.

He skimmed her face for several beats, his lips pressed together, then made a noise that sounded like encouragement.

But Poppy was suddenly shy.

'That night…'

'Which night?'

But he knew. Of course he did. 'At my party.'

'Ah. The night we had sex?'

He was being deliberately brazen. Her cheeks flooded with colour. 'Please don't talk like that here.'

'We're supposed to be dating. You don't think your boyfriend should mention S-E-X around you?'

Her cheeks grew hotter. 'You're *not* my boyfriend,' she hissed, even though they were alone.

He lifted a hand in mock surrender. 'This was your idea.'

'Yes, and I'm already regretting it,' she muttered, closing her eyes and inhaling deeply, for strength.

'What about the other night?' he asked, suddenly serious.

'I didn't… I don't know if I thought that was going to happen. But what I really wanted, what I really wanted to *know*,' she corrected, 'is why you kissed me the other time.'

'Which other time?'

Her heart stammered. He hadn't forgotten. She *knew* he hadn't forgotten because she'd mentioned it again at her twenty-fourth birthday. 'You know which night.'

'Yes,' he agreed after a moment, eyes dropping heavily to her lips.

'You followed me to the rose garden. You pulled me against you and you…you kissed me. Why?'

Without intending it, Poppy had leaned forward, her body so close to Adrastos's their faces were only an inch apart.

'Why do you think, Poppy?'

'I don't know. I've wondered ever since. Was

it because I'm a woman and you're, well, you? Had you been drinking? Were you bored?'

His lips tugged to the side. 'Perhaps it was all of those reasons.'

Poppy's eyes dropped to the console between them, her brows knitted together. She didn't want him to read the disappointment in her face. She couldn't make sense of it herself.

'That was a mistake too.'

She needed to change the subject before she said something stupid, like how much she'd liked being kissed by him, how much she'd liked sleeping with him, how no other man had ever made her feel even a hint of what he did. 'I hate the idea of this.'

His eyes roamed her face and, while it felt as though he was looking right into her soul, she had no idea what he was thinking or feeling. 'It will be over soon.'

'I'm so angry at whoever took those photos.'

'It's not their fault.'

'Then whose fault is it?' she demanded, disagreeing with him entirely.

'Mine.'

'Yours?'

'Of course.'

'Why? You didn't sell those pictures to the tabloids.'

'But I erred, Poppy. I was indiscreet. I should not have kissed you like that, there, of all places.'

'You couldn't have known—'

'Yes, I could. Don't forget, I've had a lifetime of having my every move monitored. I shouldn't have let this happen.'

Poppy's lips pulled to the side. Perhaps he was right. Unlike Poppy, Adrastos had bags of experience with living a very public life. 'Then why did you?'

His eyes probed hers, his features a mask of iron. 'Does that matter now? The point is, I should have been more guarded. Kissing you in the first place was a bad idea, but to do so at a party—it's unforgivable.'

Her heart twisted.

There was some logic to what he was saying but Poppy hated hearing him describe the kiss in that way.

'I asked you…'

'And I could have said no.'

The palace staff were waiting by the doors. Poppy's stomach was in knots. 'Forget about it. Let's just…get this over with.'

He put a hand on her thigh, and she almost jumped out of her skin. 'Poppy.' His voice held a warning. 'You can't look like a deer in the headlights every time we touch.'

She stared at his hand, tanned, large, strong,

commanding, and remembered the way it had felt for him to touch her body, to slide his fingers inside her, to pleasure her so skilfully, and felt as if the air were being dragged from her lungs.

He was right. She had to make this more natural, but that was hard to contemplate when he was capable of setting her on fire with the lightest of touches.

He lifted his hand to her chin, tilting her face towards his and, just like the deer in headlights he'd accused her of being, she stayed perfectly still, incapable of movement.

'Are you about to kiss me?'

His eyes showed surprise. 'Yes.'

'Why?'

'You need to relax.'

'I don't think kissing you will relax me.'

'Let's see,' he murmured, moving closer, his lips brushing hers, so Poppy's eyes flared wider and she looked at him for one terrified moment before her eyes swept shut and she found herself leaning further forward, inviting the kiss. For the benefit of whoever might be watching, she told herself reassuringly as her lips parted and she held her breath.

It was a totally different kiss from any they'd shared before. On previous occasions, his mouth had taken hers as if driven by the fires of passion, but now, he kissed her slowly, gently, tentatively, a kiss of idle exploration and inquiry, a kiss that unfurled desire in her belly like a snake stretching on a hot rock, rather than a torrent of lava, but desire was there, nonetheless. As his tongue flicked hers, she moaned, leaning further forward, hands lifting to his shirt, fingers bunching the fabric together, mind in tangles as she tried to cling to reality, to remember that this was fake, even as her body's response was very, very real.

He pulled away, eyes glinting with purpose as they met hers and held. 'Are you ready?'

Was she imagining the throaty quality to his voice? The huskiness?

'I think so.'

He nodded his head once, the implied approval doing something to Poppy's heart.

She tried not to take it as anything other than it was, a gesture of agreement, but her insides trembled and she experienced a little burst of something a bit like a shooting star in the cavity of her chest, an unfamiliar sensation of pleasure lightening her heart.

'Yes, I'm ready,' she said breathily. 'Let's go.'

CHAPTER FIVE

USUALLY POPPY SAT beside Eleanor at the dinner table, with the King and Queen at either end. When Adrastos was in the palace he took one end, and Queen Clementine moved to sit opposite Ellie and Poppy. Tonight, Adrastos had been placed beside Poppy, Eleanor and Clementine opposite, and a watchful King Alexander at the head.

Watchful because he didn't believe their relationship was real? Or because he didn't trust Adrastos not to hurt Poppy?

Poppy flicked a glance at her best friend, guilt assaulting her in waves whenever she contemplated the lie they were telling. But Eleanor had no idea: she was as happy as always, her love for Christmas evident in the joy she showed at this time of year, on a snowy Christmas night in the stunning royal Palace.

Champagne glasses were brought to the table, filled with ice-cold, fizzing liquid. Poppy took a quick sip of hers, even before a toast could be made, because she needed something to calm her fractured nerves.

She replaced it quickly, tilted her face and caught Adrastos watching her, his expression unreadable, but somewhere near 'thunder' on the scale of faces and moods. She lifted a brow, questioningly, and he winced out a smile—the kind of smile that would freeze ice.

Suddenly, it occurred to her that pulling this off would be harder than she'd realised. He'd said they'd need to be convincing, but he was acting as if he were heading in for a root canal.

'Well.' Alexander's voice broke the awkward silence. 'Here we are. Family.'

Poppy's eyes shifted now to Queen Clementine, whose smile was bittersweet, and then to the empty chair at the head of the table, where, in an alternate reality, Nicholas would have sat. His absence was, as always, everywhere.

'To family,' Clementine echoed.

'And new beginnings,' Eleanor drawled with a single arched brow. Poppy's heart pumped fast.

'Yes.' Clementine turned to the supposedly happy couple.

But there was a hint of doubt in her voice, a look of worry around her eyes, as if she had major reservations about this too. Poppy sipped her champagne again. They'd decided to play out this ruse and so they had to make it a success.

Beneath the table, she pressed her hand to Adrastos's thigh and, despite what he'd said in the car only an hour earlier, it was he who flinched at her touch, his powerful leg reacting to the simple, meaningless contact. She squeezed his thigh, hard, and shot him a warning look.

She was trying to show that she was in control, but when he placed his hand over hers, then laced their fingers together, any possibility of being in control fell by the wayside. How could anyone *ever* control this absolute torrent of sensation?

Awareness made her skin prickle; she turned away from him quickly, cheeks warm, reaching for her champagne with gratitude and taking several quick gulps. Beneath the table, Adrastos squeezed her hand but she refused to look at him again.

Though she'd eaten at this table many times, something had changed, and now Poppy saw it almost as an outsider, noticing the elaborate decorations that ran down the centre, the palace staff posted like sentries around the room, making genuine conversation difficult. She'd never felt that before, but the speculation from recent days had reminded her of just how highly watched this family was—and now, Poppy.

She knew from Eleanor how oppressive that could be, but Eleanor was highly adept at living her own life regardless of the press intrusion. And for the most part, as second in line to the throne and someone who had kept a low profile, there wasn't much interest in her. Unlike Adrastos, who'd made an art form of his bachelor ways.

Alexander and Clementine did most of the talking, reminding Poppy of how wonderful it had been to come to this place, where for all they were royal, they were so *normal*, reminding her of her own parents, of what real family should be like. The grief they'd endured, when Nicholas had died, had seemed to make family time even more important to the King and Queen.

Except, Adrastos had fought that.

He'd pulled away when they'd drawn closer.

Poppy had noticed, and she'd wondered, but now something had shifted and the curiosity she felt was no longer a background hum, so much as a rattling at the very front of her brain, demanding answers.

Why had he pulled away?

Why had they let him?

'Poppy?' She blinked, looking at Eleanor first and then Adrastos, who had said her name and was looking at her with a smile that didn't quite reach his eyes, his arm along the back of her chair in a perfect imitation of relaxed intimacy. It made her shiver a little, because it was fake, but for a moment she let herself imagine what it would be like if this were real.

If Adrastos were actually her boyfriend. If *she* were his girlfriend.

It was a treacherous thought, the reality so far removed from a real relationship, she couldn't even go there.

'I'm sorry, did I miss something?'

'My parents were asking if you'd like to join us at the hospital tomorrow.'

Poppy's eyes were huge. It was a visit the royal family made on the day after Christmas every year, to a children's hospital in the city. They spent hours meeting with families, children, doctors, handing out small gifts to each child on the ward.

It wasn't something Poppy had ever attended.

'Given the publicity surrounding your relationship,' Clementine said gently, 'it makes sense. It's well known that you're very much a part of our family, and, as you're now dating, the public will anticipate your attendance.'

'Oh.' A lump formed in her throat. Lying to his family was bad enough, but having to go around as his girlfriend in public? She shook her head slowly. Why hadn't she foreseen this? 'I understand what you're saying, but I don't think so.'

'Why not?' This was Adrastos, his fingers moving from the back of her chair to her shoulder, brushing her flesh slowly, rhythmically, so warmth spread through her, making thought difficult.

Poppy bit down on her lip, thinking quickly, knowing she had to control the narrative. 'We had no intention of our relationship becoming so public so soon. We wanted to take things slowly, you see. We're mindful of how complicated things are, given my relationship with your family.' She didn't look at Adrastos, but she was pleased with the way her explanation was sounding—so rational and measured. 'The story's out there now, but I don't think we need to further fan the flames. You should all carry on as normal, and I'll do the same.'

'But it's not normal,' Eleanor said with a lift of her shoulders. 'The whole world knows you're an item. So what harm could come from spending time together publicly? You've done nothing wrong.'

Hadn't they?

'Poppy's right.' It was Adrastos, and his support was like steel in her backbone. She felt it flood her and breathed out, relaxing. 'There will be other hospital visits, other festive seasons. We do not need to rush anything.'

Poppy's breath hitched in her throat at the ease with which he lied—and the convincing nature of it. He made it sound as if it were a foregone conclusion that they would still be together this time next year, and the one after that. She almost believed him! She caught the surprised, happy look that Clementine and Eleanor exchanged and almost died with mortification. This was a terrible lie she'd been caught up in—a necessity of circumstance. It didn't make it any easier to sit across from these people and deceive them.

'The offer is there, should you change your mind, Poppy darling. You know we think of you as one of our own.'

She could only hope that was still the case when all this was over.

Nothing in the palace had ever been off limits to Poppy. From the minute she'd arrived, she'd been welcomed with open arms and told to think of the place quite as her own home. Eleanor had taken her under her wing and together they'd explored every nook and cranny, running through the beautiful, ancient, elegant corridors, some with parquetry floors, some with marble, all with high ceilings, gold vaulted, and enormous floral arrangements on every single piece of furniture. The palace itself dated back to the twelfth century, the oldest parts of it having been refurbished in the rococo style hundreds of years ago, so they were incredibly ornate and breathtaking.

There were only two areas she'd avoided, and

not because anyone had ever said as much, but because Eleanor had avoided them and Poppy had understood. They'd never gone anywhere near Nicholas's room, nor had they approached Adrastos's.

The former because it was too hard for Eleanor, who'd only been thirteen when her oldest brother had died. The latter because he was someone who seemed to demand, without ever saying as much, that his privacy be respected.

They'd been girls when Poppy had arrived—just fourteen—and Adrastos a man of nineteen. He was intimidating and frightening, silent, strong, brooding and powerful. Even Eleanor had been a little afraid of him.

He's not like Nicholas. Nicholas was gentle and soft. I could tell him what I wanted to do and he would always go along with it, never mind that I was so much younger. Adrastos is...scary.

Silently, Poppy had disagreed. He wasn't scary, so much as intimidating. There was a vital difference. Scary implied something negative, whereas to Poppy it had always seemed that Adrastos was simply too much of everything. Too smart, too powerful, too strong, too athletic, too handsome by a mile, and so it was difficult to be oneself around him.

And so it was that despite having spent years living in the palace, after dinner, Adrastos guided her to a part of it that was wholly unfamiliar, through a wide set of double doors she'd never crossed, into a corridor with one door on either side.

'My office,' he explained, waving a hand to the left. 'And my room.' His eyes held hers for a moment too long, as though he was hesitating or working out what else he could say, then he pushed the door inwards and stood just inside, waiting for Poppy.

Her nerves were stretched, her heart racing, blood washing through her ears as loud and urgent as the ocean on a stormy night, but Adrastos was watching her, and waiting, and she didn't feel as though she could simply hover on the threshold.

'This is weird,' she said on an apologetic half-smile, thinking longingly of her own room, just down from Ellie's, the familiar view over the rose garden.

'A little.' He dipped his head forward in agreement, still waiting, so she sucked in a breath and pushed forward, step after step, into his room, looking first at Adrastos and then quickly away when their eyes met and she felt as if she were losing her footing.

His room was big, and she expelled a breath of relief. More than spacious enough for the two of them.

She took a few more steps, towards the bed, then froze. The bed.

It was right there. Huge. Reminding her of another bed, in a faraway penthouse.

She spun abruptly, almost bumping into Adrastos, who was so close she could have reached out and touched him. Her heart was in overdrive.

'I—'

What?

What could she say in that moment? Everything was spinning completely out of control.

'I think they believed us.'

'It would not occur to any of them that we would lie. Not about this.'

That was an indictment, if ever she'd heard one. 'I hate that we're doing this.'

'There is no sense discussing that now. We've made our choice.'

So final. So simple. Could he really be so clear-cut about something so complicated? Perhaps that was a secret to his strength: no ambivalence. Poppy, perhaps through her legal training, saw everything through every facet.

Adrastos moved away from Poppy, towards a door. 'There's a bathroom there, a kitchen, a lounge. Obviously you should feel free to call staff for anything you require.'

Poppy wrinkled her nose. She rarely availed herself of the palace servants. Though she'd come to live here and been treated as one of the family, she knew she *wasn't* actually an Aetos, and hadn't wanted to ever seem to be taking things for granted.

'Do you mind if I make a tea?'

'Not at all. So long as you don't mind if I have something a little stronger,' he responded with a tight smile.

She toyed with her hands. 'Of course not.'

They stared at each other for several beats.

'I was—'

'Do you—?'

They spoke at the same time, so Poppy lifted a hand to her throat and pulled a face. 'Please. What were you saying?'

He gestured to the door of the kitchen, and Poppy was relieved to move that way, relieved to have something practical to focus on, instead of the inherent discomfort afforded by this circumstance.

'You did well tonight,' he said, and she had no idea if it was what he'd intended to say or not but, either way, the praise warmed her heart.

'So did you.'

The kitchen was luxurious and well appointed, but not enormous—like something in a five-star hotel, she thought, moving behind the bar and filling the kettle. Adrastos went to a liquor cabinet and removed a bottle with a label Poppy didn't recognise, pouring a generous measure into a crystal glass before turning to face her, bracing his hip on the edge of the counter.

She made a tea, watching as the water darkened, then lifted her gaze to him, uncertainty holding her silent, but curiosity finally pushed her to speak. 'How come you're the way you are?'

He pulled a face, perhaps intentionally misunderstanding her. 'Tall? Dark? Handsome?'

Her lips tugged to one side in an unconscious sign of amusement. 'All of the above,' she agreed with a little wrinkle of her brow. 'But that's not what I meant.'

'No? Then what are you asking?'

She sighed. 'With women,' she blurted out, catching her by surprise. 'How come you don't date?'

His eyes were locked to hers but there was nothing in them. No hint of feeling, no suggestion of an explanation. He was so good at hiding his innermost thoughts! 'Does it matter?'

She pulled a face. 'I'm not sure.'

'Then let me tell you: it doesn't.'

'I'm curious, though.'

'Why?'

'Because you're old enough to be married,' she pointed out. 'And it's certainly expected of you.'

'Eleanor will marry.'

Poppy tilted her head to the side, considering that. 'Are you saying you don't see it as your role to marry and have heirs?'

'Not necessarily. However, should I fail in that area, Eleanor's children may inherit the throne. I do not consider it my birthright, nor do I consider my children the sole heirs to the responsibility.'

Poppy's lips parted, her mind swimming. She hadn't expected such frankness, but his answers were deeply unsatisfying, for everything he said only made her want to know more.

He was a riddle, complex and ever changing.

And then, he was moving towards her, pacing slowly, yet there didn't seem to be enough time to brace for his nearness.

'I am much more interested in your relationship history, or lack thereof,' he said with a gentleness to his voice that might have been a reproach.

She shook her head, unable to think anything approaching straight because of his proximity. 'I—there's nothing to tell.'

'I beg to differ. A twenty-four-year-old virgin is not exactly commonplace.'

She frowned. 'Gee, thanks.'

He shrugged. 'It's the truth. Would you prefer me to lie?'

'I would prefer not to talk about it.'

'Are you embarrassed? Ashamed?'

'No, and definitely not.'

'I am glad to hear it.'

'But it's personal.'

'You tricked me into taking your virginity.'

'I did not trick you!'

His nostrils flared but otherwise he didn't react. 'We were both there. You had a chance to tell me; you didn't.' She couldn't refute that. He was right; they both knew what had happened that night. 'Don't I deserve some explanation?'

She closed her eyes and he moved closer, his body so strong and warm, and even though it was his questions filling her with uncertainty, he was also the antidote to that, so she wanted to lean against him and draw strength and courage from his powerful frame.

'Damn it, Adrastos,' she groaned, blinking up at him.

As if he understood what she needed, he closed every last skerrick of distance between them, his eyes half mocking, half sensual, when they held hers.

She chewed on her lower lip, shaking her head. 'It's not a big deal. I've just never had sex before.'

Standing so close, he now lifted a hand to tuck some hair behind her ear, the touch gentle and light, before falling to her shoulder. She almost jumped at the contact. 'You went to a co-ed school. Then university. You have a job, in an office, with, I presume, other people. You have lived away from the palace since you were eighteen years old. There has been no shortage of opportunities, and I am sure no shortage of willing and available men throwing themselves at your feet…'

'If they were, I didn't notice.'

'Oh, come on. You're not seriously saying you've never noticed how men look at you?'

Her pulse throbbed heavily in her veins. 'What are you talking about? You've never seen me with men.'

'But I've seen *you*, and I am a man. I know that any red-blooded male would find it hard to be around you and not wonder…'

'Don't say that.' She squeezed her eyes shut against his compliment. It wasn't, couldn't be, true. Not of him, and not of anyone. 'I know you don't feel that way.'

'I understand that you're inexperienced but you were there the other night, weren't you? You saw the effect you have on me.'

'I thought it was a mistake?'

'It was a mistake to act on my attraction but that doesn't change how I felt.'

She shook her head, sipping her tea quickly, and burning her tongue. 'Damn it.' Her voice shook a little. She placed her tea down quickly. 'Just…stop.'

'I can't understand why this is an issue.'

'Because I'm not—I don't—I mean, I've been asked out. I'm just…'

His eyes had an intensity that made her realise he was paying very close attention, not just to her words but to what she wasn't saying as well. He moved his hand lower, down her arm, to her wrist. Goosebumps trailed in the wake of his touch.

'You've been asked out, and?'

And any of the dates she'd gone on had been abysmal failures, because she'd treated them almost like job interviews. It had been of little interest to her before her twenty-first, but after that kiss, something had shifted inside Poppy, had been completely closed off, so she couldn't think of a man without remembering the way Adrastos had made her feel.

'I've been busy, Adrastos,' she said, unevenly. 'Law school, my job—'

'Not so busy you couldn't date.'

'We weren't all born to be playboy princes,' she said with an attempt at dismissive humour she immediately regretted, because she knew he hated the moniker the press had given him. He wasn't a playboy. He was intelligent and focussed on his role as Prince; he just happened to see a lot of women in his downtime.

'Somewhere between my lifestyle and yours there is a happy medium,' he said, his voice gruff, so she couldn't help but tilt her face towards his, to see him better. Then wished she hadn't when their eyes locked and she felt that powerful, zapping connection.

Her heart stammered and she swallowed unevenly.

'When I kissed you,' he said slowly, moving his hand to the small of her back and pressing her forward lightly, so their bodies were melded. He smelled of cologne and Scotch. Her stomach rolled.

'Which time?' she asked, aiming for tart and instead sounding breathless.

'At your twenty-first birthday.' He moved his other hand to her cheek, his thumb brushing the corner of her mouth. She closed her eyes on an uneven breath.

'Yes?'

'Was that your first kiss?'

Her eyes flew open. She should have been prepared for the question. Mortification at her inexperience was making her toes crawl.

'Answer me,' he demanded, moving his thumb further over her lower lip, tracing the outline, and a thousand fireworks ignited in her bloodstream. She was mesmerised, quite possibly hypnotised by him. In that moment, she would have answered him anything, *given* him anything.

'Yes,' she muttered, gaze held locked to his.

'Am I the only man to ever kiss you, Poppy?'

Slowly, careful not to dislodge his thumb, because she liked being this close to him, loved being touched by him so intimately, she shifted her head once, in something like a nod. So what if he knew the truth? Did it really matter?

She couldn't interpret the emotions that swirled in the depths of his eyes, the colour shifting, his expression changing infinitesimally, but she felt a burst of something like restlessness, of need, something unfamiliar wrestling inside her.

'Poppy.' He said her name slowly, as though it were a thing of great wonder, and then, slowly, giving her plenty of time to anticipate his intention, and even more time to move if she wanted to, he lowered his head, his eyes probing hers with confusion and disbelief, until his hand fell away from her mouth a short moment before his lips claimed that space. The only man who'd ever kissed her and he kissed her now as though he wanted to read her, to understand her, with his mouth alone. Poppy whimpered as the beast inside her thrashed and turned and her body grew white-hot and she wanted, more than anything, to growl or cry. She couldn't understand why she felt the way she did, but the energy bursting through her veins was strong enough to power a small country.

She mumbled his name into Adrastos's mouth, and then he lifted her, placing her on the edge of the kitchen bench and standing between her legs, making him a better height to explore her mouth, his hands on her hips at first then falling behind her, bringing her forward, all the while he kissed her and she wanted to surrender completely, to lie back then and there and have him take her once more.

He was the only man she'd ever kissed. The only man she'd ever made love to, but the same could not be said for Adrastos. He slept with women all the time. None of this meant anything to him. He was very, very skilled at turning women's bones to mush, just like this. It was an art form for him, going through the motions, not special, not unique.

It was meaningless. Just as the other night had been.

If Poppy hadn't been a virgin, if someone hadn't snapped photos and sold them for a nice little pay day, they wouldn't be doing this.

He was just making the most of the situation, of having her there, and she was going along with it because she had no experience and even less self-control.

With a sharp groan, she pulled away from him, wiping her mouth with the back of her hand as though by erasing his kiss she could jolt herself out of the sensual fog.

'I'm not going to sleep with you just because we're sharing a room,' she said bravely, eyes clouded with uncertainty, but she tilted her chin to make that point.

Adrastos was also confused, she could see, but he rallied faster, concealing his emotions with far greater ease. 'That wasn't sex, Poppy, it was a kiss.'

Heat bloomed in her cheeks. What a perfect comment to make Poppy feel every bit as gauche and inexperienced as she was.

'Yes, well, I don't want you to do either,' she lied. 'Would you please step aside so I can get down?'

She couldn't meet his eyes.

The last thing she was expecting was Adrastos's gentle touch as he moved his hands back to her hips and lifted her off the bench, bringing her against his body until her feet were back on the kitchen floor.

The wild beast inside Poppy had stilled, was watching, waiting to see what would happen next.

'What is it?'

Of course he could tell something was wrong.

One minute she'd been kissing him back as though her life depended on it and the next she was barely able to look at him.

'Nothing.' She shook her head. How could she explain her strange, amorphous jealousy? Of the women he'd been with, of his confidence with women, of his skill…

At her birthday party, she'd wanted him in spite of all those things, perhaps because of them, but the intimacy of their new arrangement had bred a wariness in Poppy, and a warning, too. It would be impossible to relegate this experience with Adrastos to 'just another guy', as he would easily do with her, because she had no point of comparison, no other experience.

In Poppy's work, she dealt with injustice every day, she worked with people who'd been in situations of inherent unfairness and power imbalance, which made it easy for Poppy to identify that here. The idea of wanting him with her whole soul, and knowing that, for Adrastos, Poppy was just someone to keep his bed warm because they had to share a room, made it all the more imperative for Poppy to draw and maintain some boundaries, or else she'd lose herself in this entirely.

'I'm going to bed.' Her glare was an attempt at a warning, and nothing that could be construed as an invitation. 'Goodnight.'

CHAPTER SIX

SHE HAD SLEPT like a log, despite the tumult of the day and that moment in the kitchen. She'd passed out almost as soon as her head had hit the pillow, but then, at some point, she'd become aware of Adrastos beside her, and then Poppy had been wide awake, the beast in her chest doing laps, pacing around, desperate for Poppy to *do something.*

'Do you need a sleeping tablet?'

His voice broke through the silence and she flipped her head towards his without thinking—an act that brought their faces within a couple of inches. In the silver light of the night, his features were shadowed and somehow more impressive.

'Why?'

'You have been tossing and turning for hours. Are you always such an animated sleeper?'

'I wouldn't know,' she responded, squeezing her eyes shut in a very poor facsimile of sleep.

He sighed then was silent, his breathing rhythmic once more. Poppy turned onto her side and stared at the windows. Adrastos did not have a view of the rose gardens, like Eleanor and Poppy. His room overlooked the other side of the palace, a wooded area that was wild and ancient. As a boy, he used to go hunting in there, with his father and brother. Poppy knew this because Eleanor had told her with a sniff of disapproval as they'd researched animal welfare groups online and planned all the ways in which they'd outlaw hunting if ever they had the opportunity. They had been sixteen and idealistic.

In the darkness, Poppy could see the enormous trees silhouetted against the night sky, and her eyes chased the tops of the trees for a long time, her heart twisting, her mind gnarled and overactive, her every breath making her aware of the other occupant of this bed, his breaths, his nearness…

She groaned softly, then flipped onto her back, tapping her fingers on her stomach.

'I can't sleep,' she whispered, so quietly that if he was still asleep, he wouldn't have heard.

But his response was immediate. 'Evidently.'

'It's your fault. Everything's different. I feel weird.'

Another sigh.

'You are the one who suggested this.'

'I know.'

She frowned, looking at him again. Was he annoyed at her about that? She'd acted on instinct, terrified of losing this family that had taken her in when she'd been at her lowest ebb. But that had completely changed his life—at least for the next twelve nights. How did he feel about that?

'Turn onto your side.'

She hesitated. 'Why?'

'Because if you don't sleep, I won't be able to either and I have a full schedule tomorrow. Roll over.'

'What are you going to do?' she asked, but as she spoke she did as he'd said, flipping onto one side.

The bed dipped as he moved closer. Her heart almost gave out. 'Close your eyes.' His tone was hoarse. A moment later, his finger pressed to the centre of her back, pausing there a moment before moving in a slow, steady figure of eight. A shuddered breath fell from between her lips.

'Oh.'

'Keep your eyes closed.'

She did as he said, but with every swish of his finger, something shifted inside her, a growing bundle of awareness and need, so she wondered if she should tell him that his attempt to lull her was having quite the opposite effect. He was so sexy. So incredibly sexy. From the first moment she'd seen him, she'd been overpowered by his appeal, and it hit her now right between her solar plexus, so she had to fight an urge to roll over and face him, to pull him down to the mattress.

It was the last thought Poppy had before falling fast asleep, Adrastos's soothing touch at her back continuing for a long time afterwards, his hands roaming her body on autopilot until finally he realised what he was doing and stood, staring down at the sleeping woman with consternation before slipping from the room, needing space to clear his mind.

Poppy had come into his house as a fourteen-year-old and since then she'd been a regular fixture. Regular enough that any decent man would have considered her basically a sister.

But he'd never felt that for Poppy, he realised, as he stepped into the kitchen and leaned against the fridge. He'd fought those feelings tooth and nail, even as his family had embraced her and made her an unofficial member of their clan. He'd wondered, at the time, if it was loyalty to Nick, as though everyone else was trying to replace the boy who'd been lost with a stray girl, but that didn't quite seem right. He'd held her at arm's length, and now he wondered if *this* was why. Maybe he'd always known their chemistry had the power to burn him to the core. Maybe he'd always wanted to reserve the right to explore this…

He bit back a groan of his own because no matter how he felt about Poppy, to his family she was one of theirs. He shouldn't let this go any further. They both had to make it through their relationship pretence unscathed, emerging as 'friends' when she left the country, so his family would accept the break-up with a small degree of disappointment and move on.

But hell, if he didn't want to kiss her awake and make her his. He didn't know why she'd pulled back in the kitchen. It was as though something had flicked off inside her, and the wild, whimpering woman who had been dissolving into a puddle in his arms became instead a frightened animal. And just as he would with such a creature, he'd backed off immediately, knowing that space was needed to calm her down. His own desire though had been to lean forward and kiss her back to fever pitch, which he knew he could have done easily. Which he knew he could do now.

Just knowing that he was the only man to ever stir those feelings in her spoke to some kind of ancient, male part of his soul, a part he should probably have been ashamed of. Whatever had happened between them in the kitchen, Poppy was running from it. Out of fear? Lack of experience? Nervousness?

He moved to the bench where she'd sat and pressed a finger against it. Heat travelled from his fingertips to his shoulder then spread through his chest. He closed his eyes and breathed in; his lips almost tingled with the memories of kissing her, and then he frowned, because he couldn't remember the last time he'd given a woman this much space in his head, if ever.

For Adrastos, the end of this pretence, and Poppy's departure from Stomland, couldn't come soon enough.

Poppy couldn't help herself. The day after Christmas, while the royal family was at the hospital, she found herself watching the coverage on the national station, and when the reporters approached the Aetos family outside the hospital, almost all the questions were about Adrastos's love life. It was quite remarkable how he tolerated the invasive remarks without flinching, answering with a practised deflection, turning attention back to the hospital whenever he could. It was a masterclass in PR.

Nonetheless, it was apparent to Poppy that her own life was going to be altered by this.

Even after their purported break-up, there'd probably continue to be a level of interest surrounding her that might even make it difficult to tackle her work in the usual way. Should she at least make contact with the HR department of her law firm, to explain the situation?

To explain *what*? she thought with a grimace. To broaden this bloody lie? To more people?

She was under no obligation to disclose personal details to her work. Surely they'd have seen the reports like every other person in the world. It wouldn't impact her job performance—she wouldn't let it—so there was no problem there. But she didn't relish the idea of going about her business with a paparazzi entourage.

Surely it would only take a week or so, after they broke up, before the press bored of her. The interest would be in Adrastos, and his next quarry. He wouldn't be single long. Then that woman would become the object of their scrutiny.

Just the thought made Poppy's heart drop to her toes. She turned off the TV and wandered through the palace, not to Adrastos's room, but to her own. She needed a little space and clarity, and somehow the familiar outlook of the rose garden would, she hoped, calm her fluttering mind and erratic, fast-moving pulse.

It was like stepping back in time. Six weeks ago she'd been here, but she felt *different* from that Poppy. More awakened and alive. On the night of her twenty-fourth birthday, something had happened to her, and even though they were living a lie, she wasn't sure if she would change anything about this adventure. Because it was an adventure to pretend to be Adrastos's girlfriend. As if riding on a roller coaster, she felt as though she were zipping in one direction after the other the entire time, never sure what to expect.

But this was the room that centred her. She had been coming here for a decade—it was a home to Poppy. She moved to the windowsill, staring out at the beautiful garden, memories shifting through her mind.

It was lucky she'd been at the palace for a week already, on that first trip, before Adrastos had come back from military college. In that one week, she'd had a chance to fall in love with Eleanor, Clementine and Alexander. The latter had proven a balm to her broken heart with all the stories he'd told of her parents, almost making them come back to life for a grieving Poppy. Clementine had held her tight each evening, as Poppy had drunk a sweetened milk, and Eleanor had become her best friend almost instantly. They'd been so similar, like sisters separated at birth, they always joked.

They'd settled into a routine that was everything Poppy had needed. For the first time since her parents' deaths, she'd felt as though she could breathe again.

And then, just like that, Adrastos had returned.

She'd known he was coming, because his arrival had been spoken of, but she'd presumed in the older brother she'd find another family member like the three she'd come to know and love. Instead, Adrastos had exploded like a tropical storm, so powerful and big, so different, instantly changing the atmosphere, charging it with an electrical current.

He was unlike anyone Poppy had ever met.

Her brow furrowed.

She'd been awestruck, yes, but it was something else. Something more.

Without her knowledge or consent, so much of her mind had begun to focus on him. She began to wonder about him, to think about him even when he wasn't around. She was too self-conscious to ask Eleanor the million questions burning through her, and, in fact, instinctively knew she should hide her feelings from her friend. It felt illicit to fantasise about her best friend's brother, but she couldn't stop.

He never came back for long.

'He's always busy,' Clementine had said one day, a wistful smile on her beautiful face.

Poppy had felt the same wistfulness in her heart.

From that first visit onwards, she was on tenterhooks, waiting for him. Listening for him.

Those brief flashes of time, in which Adrastos would arrive and become a complete centre of gravity. When he wasn't at the palace, there was no shortage of information online about Prince Adrastos. It was a double-edged sword to search his name because so many of the stories made her heart sink.

For as long as she'd known of Adrastos, there'd been speculation about his love life. Speculation about his girlfriends, whether this one might be 'the one', whether a royal engagement was in the offing. At the time, she'd told herself that the sense of irritation she felt about those stories was because she knew how important it was to Clementine and Alexander that Adrastos settle down. She told herself it was loyalty to them, and their wishes. But what if, even then, it had been more? What if even as a teenager, that overwhelming awe she'd felt for Adrastos was actually something far more mature?

She sighed heavily, turned away from the window and the rose garden and strode out of her room, back into the wide, marbled corridor, in the direction of the suite she was sharing with Adrastos.

She'd manoeuvred this; all of it. Not intentionally: she would have died rather than have the whole world know something so intimate as the fact she'd slept with Adrastos. But if Poppy hadn't approached Adrastos at the party, it wouldn't have happened. If she hadn't dug her way out of Clementine's disapproval by making up a pretend relationship, then this situation would have been avoided. But she'd done both those things, and now she had to act her heart out to convince everyone this was the real deal. For the sake of her relationship with the entire family, they had to pull this off.

CHAPTER SEVEN

'OH!'

She started as he entered, so it occurred to Adrastos, belatedly, that he should probably have knocked. While technically it was his room, they weren't really a couple, and it was natural that Poppy should expect some privacy during this twelve-day sojourn.

Not that it had been anything like a sojourn, and it had only just begun.

Exhaustion seeped through Adrastos—an unfamiliar emotion for a man who could run on air.

'Did I disturb you?' he asked, unable to stop his eyes from slowly roaming her body, from the top of her darkly shining hair to her slender shoulders and generous breasts, lower to her neat waist and curved hips, slim legs, dainty feet. His gut tightened in unwelcome response. She wore a pair of jeans and a long-sleeved T-shirt, fitted and a little too short, so it revealed just the smallest hint of midriff, reminding him of how soft her skin had been, like a rose petal. That did very little to help the tightening of his body.

'I wasn't expecting you,' she said with a murmur, putting down an iPad and turning to face him. 'I was just catching up on some work.'

That interested him—Poppy worked hard, she always had. And now, she'd earned a promotion that would take her to the place where human rights law was, largely, written. She had every right to be proud of that.

He moved past Poppy even as his body was doing its best to drag him to her, into the kitchen, where he opened the fridge and removed a bottle of mineral water. He held one in her direction.

She shook her head. 'I have tea, thank you.'

'I thought you were on holiday?'

'I am, technically. But my to-do list is about this high.' She waved one hand way above her head. 'I figured I could get a jump on it during my spare time. How was the hospital?'

The conversation change was swift and frustrating, because he found he had more questions about her work, her life. He was curious as to how she filled her days, now that it was abundantly clear she had no social life.

'Fine,' he said, frowning. 'Difficult.' The admission surprised Adrastos. It was something he hadn't ever remarked even to his parents, despite the fact they did this every year.

Poppy's face crumpled a little with a soft sympathy. She was very beautiful. As a teenager, there'd been something unsettling about her. Those huge brown eyes, so big they could almost have been digitally enhanced, full, curving lips, and a watchful nature that had made him feel uncomfortable and somehow wrong—a feeling Adrastos had never otherwise felt. As she'd grown up, her face had changed. She'd grown into her features, but the watchfulness was still there, that same sense that Poppy saw far more than anyone else, that she processed everything carefully before passing judgment.

'It must bring back a lot of memories.'

He tightened his grip on the mineral water. A perfect image of Nicholas, smiling, came to Adrastos and his throat was suddenly lined with razor blades. 'I've made plans for us tonight.'

She blinked at him, the answer obviously the last thing she was expecting.

'Oh.' She looked down at her iPad, face averted for far longer than it took to press the off button, so he knew she was taking a moment to conceal her emotions. Frustration chomped through him.

'Unless that's a problem?' His tone was sharper than he'd intended, but he didn't like how clearly she understood him, nor how quickly he'd confided in her. Even that one word—*difficult*—had been too much.

'I—well, why?'

'Why?'

'Why should we go out? Isn't the point of this to convince your parents and sister we're the real deal?'

'And ask yourself this: would I really expect any girlfriend of mine to sit around the palace for twelve days straight, without a little fun thrown in?'

'But I'm not any girlfriend,' Poppy pointed out. 'I'm like family to your family. I don't mind if we stay here the whole time.'

'Well, I do. It doesn't ring true and my parents will see that.'

She pulled her lips to the side, considering that.

'So where would we go?'

'Does it matter?'

She scrunched her face. 'I'm a planner.'

'So much of a planner that you've hesitated your way out of a sex life?'

She flinched and he regretted the comment—which hadn't been intended cruelly. He was simply struggling—still—to understand how she'd missed such an important part of her development.

'You don't know what you're talking about.'

'So enlighten me.'

'No.'

He arched a brow. 'You do realise that by turning yourself into a challenge, you're making me want to win?'

He saw the way she shivered, her eyes almost pleading with his. 'There's nothing to win. My love life is none of your business.'

Frustration arced through him, but it wasn't necessary to push this now. They had more than enough time together to explore the matter at his leisure. 'Can you be ready in an hour?'

Poppy stared at him with obvious consternation. 'Are you serious?'

'Of course.'

She hesitated, and he could see that she was torn between agreeing and fighting. Eventually, common sense won out.

'Fine,' she murmured. 'But only in the service of this ruse.'

He moved closer to Poppy, eyes sparking with hers, relishing this chance to be close to her, even just for a moment. 'Exactly as it should be, *deliciae*.'

He pressed a kiss to the tip of her nose, then, unsatisfied with such a pointless, insufficient contact, yanked Poppy hard against his body and took her mouth, claiming it with all the desperate, angry, sad, needy emotions that had been pummelling him all day. Suddenly, he saw the chasm of pain in his chest, saw it as it always was: a part of him. But he saw an antidote, a solution: Poppy. When he kissed her, that pain became almost bearable, and for a moment, he forgot. Forgot that he was only the spare. That none of this should have been his. Forgot that he was walking through life in another man's shoes, forgot the survivor guilt that dogged him mercilessly, so that he was simply a man, making love to a woman.

'Adrastos,' she groaned into his mouth, lifting one leg and wrapping it around his hips, desperately trying to be closer to him so he felt her groan deep in his soul because what he wanted, more than anything, was to strip her naked and finish what they'd started last night. He pushed his hands into her hair, pulling it from the messy bun she'd scraped it into, drawing her head back so he could kiss her more, so he could devour her, kissing her until she was almost whimpering and she was grinding her hips in a rhythm that spoke of hunger and need, wanting him to take her, offering herself to him as much now as she had that night.

It terrified him, how much he wanted her. How much he wanted to forget her part in his family, how much he wanted to remove her from his family so she was just *his*. Was this what had stopped her last night? Had she also felt some kind of shock at the strength of their connection?

As though he'd been burned, he pulled away from her quickly, doing his best to assume a cynical expression. 'You definitely look the part now.'

Her eyes were hooded, her face flushed, her lips swollen from where he'd been sucking and pressing them, her body trembling, her nipples taut through the flimsy cotton of her shirt. He took in the picture of her and committed it to memory because she was the most beautiful and sexy woman he'd ever seen. But her eyes blinked in confusion and then hurt and shame and he felt the strangest feeling in the pit of his stomach, his own sense of remorse.

He spun away from her only so he could move to the door.

'One hour, Poppy. I'll be back soon.'

He left the room without another word. He was too busy replaying what had just happened and wondering if he would ever be able to be alone with Poppy without losing control completely.

She'd chosen a dress that was conservative and simple, and yet somehow, perhaps because of the way Adrastos had kissed her not an hour earlier, Poppy felt distinctly...sexy. She stared at her reflection with a deep frown, her eyes taking in the image she saw in the mirror with more than a little uncertainty. She'd gone to extra effort tonight, some feminine pride insisting she really looked the part of Adrastos's girlfriend.

The dress was beautiful—bought for a film premiere a couple of years ago and stored here at the palace, with all of her most exquisite clothing. It was burgundy in colour, with a halter neck that showed off Poppy's toned arms, fitted all the way to the knees, and cinched at the waist with a belt in a matching material but with a slight pattern. The shoes were black and sky-high—fortunately, Poppy was comfortable in heels. For jewellery, Poppy had chosen a pair of pearl earrings that Clementine had given her for her sixteenth birthday.

'Your mother was with me when I got these,' Clementine had offered at the time, with a sad smile. 'In Western Australia, we visited the most exquisite pearl property on the north coast. It was a wonderful holiday, for all of us. We both bought a pair, you know. I don't know where your mother's went, but I thought you should have these. I hope you like them, Poppy darling. I know she'd be thrilled for you to wear them.'

Poppy did wear them, but only rarely, because they were so special to her, she couldn't bear to think of anything happening to them. But when she needed a little extra kick of confidence, to feel that her mother *and* fairy godmother were watching over her, the earrings were a must. And tonight definitely constituted a night for extra confidence.

Ten minutes before the hour was up, when Poppy conceded that yes, she was ready, a knock sounded at the door. Well, that was better than having him barge in. She crossed the room a little unsteadily.

This was all for show, she reminded herself, pulling the door inwards, the sharp barb she'd prepared freezing when she saw Eleanor on the other side.

'Ellie!' The relief was enormous. She threw her arms around her best friend and almost cried with relief.

Ellie laughed. 'Goodness, are you okay?'

'Yes, I'm fine. I just—I'm glad to see you.'

Eleanor pulled back a little, studying Poppy thoughtfully. 'I understand you have a date with my brother.'

Poppy bit down on her lower lip, nodding. Oh, how she hated the necessity of this lie.

'Well, that's fine, but first of all, come with me.'

'Oh.' Poppy looked over her shoulder. 'He'll be here any minute—'

'Yes, I know. I heard him making the arrangements and, believe me when I tell you, it will do Adrastos the world of good to be kept waiting.' Eleanor winked. *'Trust me,'* she said, conspiratorially. 'This is for his own good—and yours too.'

Poppy *did* trust Eleanor, and when it came to matters of the heart, there was no questioning who had more experience. 'Okay.' Poppy smiled almost her first real smile all day. 'Where are we going?'

Ten minutes later, they were ensconced in the family's favourite living room, with a beautiful Christmas tree twinkling in the flames cast by the fire, a glass of ice-cold champagne in each woman's hand, and the awkwardness of the last few days erased completely by the old, familiar routines that they'd spent a decade establishing.

They talked about Poppy's next case, and Eleanor's love life, and skirted around the issue of the hospital visit, which Poppy knew was always difficult for Eleanor as well, just as Adrastos had admitted it was for him. They talked non-stop, so that before Poppy realised it half an hour had passed and she'd finished her champagne. Eleanor had just left the room to top up their glasses when Adrastos stalked in, expression like thunder.

'I thought I asked you to wait in my room?'

Poppy's eyes flared wide and she was immediately enraged by his tone. 'Do you really think you have any right to speak to me like that, Your Highness?' she asked in a hushed whisper, standing and moving towards him with more than a spark of anger.

'We had a deal, remember?'

'No, we had a "date".' She used air quotation marks with some enjoyment. 'And you didn't do me the decency of consulting me before making plans, so you could have had no idea if I was already busy or not,' she pointed out. 'And I was.' The champagne had gone just a little to her head already.

'What plans?' he asked, and then, as if seeing her for the first time, he devoured her with his eyes, in that slow yet impatient way he had, as if he needed to visually inspect every single inch of her.

'That would be me,' Eleanor called from across the room, her smile the exact kind one sibling could reserve for the other, the smile of someone who was enjoying needling an older brother just a little too much.

Adrastos glowered.

'I'm sorry, Adrastos. Blame me. I've hardly seen Poppy since you arrived.'

'We all had lunch together earlier,' Adrastos pointed out, somehow extinguishing his temper—or the appearance of it—almost immediately.

'I mean, *just* Poppy and me.'

A muscle jerked in his jaw. 'I see. Have you had enough time together?'

'No,' Eleanor responded quickly, even as Poppy was already moving to collect her handbag. 'Now I'd like to spend time with both of you. Please, take a seat.'

Poppy laughed softly. 'Ellie, you're making it sound like an interview.'

'I'm curious,' she said with a lift of her shoulders. 'Indulge me.'

Poppy threw Adrastos a look, wanting him to whisk them away, but his features now bore a mask of resignation. He moved to a small sofa, took a seat then gestured with his head for Poppy to take the space beside him. Only it was *not* a large sofa at all and Adrastos, with his bulky macho warrior's frame, took up considerably more than half of it, meaning it was almost impossible to imagine being able to squeeze herself into the seat without touching him.

But the alternative was to choose a different seat and, given that they were trying to convince Eleanor their relationship was the real deal, Poppy had no option but to go and sit beside Adrastos. She perched her bottom on the edge of the cushions. Adrastos leaned forward, pressing a kiss to her exposed shoulder, whispering so that only she could hear, 'Relax.'

Not likely.

And made almost impossible when he brought an arm to her shoulders and pulled her back a little, positioning her against his body, his arm draped with casual possession around, his fingers grazing the top of her breast so her whole body was an electrical live wire. She drew in a shuddering breath and turned to face him. Eleanor was distracted by the music, changing from an upbeat Christmas song to a slower classic, so Poppy took advantage of that and leaned towards Adrastos, whispering, 'What are you doing?'

'You want to play games? I'm going to play them right back.'

His smile was wolfish and Poppy's body lifted with goosebumps. She didn't doubt him. 'What games?'

'Keeping me waiting?'

She bit down on her lip, eyes shifting betrayingly to Eleanor.

'Ah,' he murmured, moving his lips closer to her shoulder. 'Let me guess. It was my sister's idea.'

Loyalty kept Poppy quiet. She sniffed slightly and looked away, but Adrastos was not an easy man to ignore.

He moved his body so it almost engulfed hers, so big and broad was he, and Poppy couldn't breathe without tasting him and smelling him and feeling him in every single one of her senses.

'So.' Eleanor looked up from her phone and took a seat opposite, looking relaxed except for the glint in her eye. 'Tell me about this.' She gestured from one to the other.

'I—' Poppy faltered, her heart dropping. Oh, how she hated lying! To anyone, but especially Eleanor. Why, oh, why had she ever thought a fake relationship was a good idea?

'This?' Adrastos repeated, moving his fingers ever so slightly, so Poppy couldn't help but be aware of the building of tension, the frisson of awareness rocketing through her. 'It's a relationship, Eleanor. You might have heard of the concept? When two people decide they'd like to get to know one another better, in a romantic sense, and commit to going on a series of dates?'

'I know you're more than familiar with the concept,' Eleanor volleyed back witheringly, with no idea of how hurtful that observation would have been to Poppy were this relationship genuine. 'I mean, specifically, you two. How did it happen?'

He sighed. 'Is this a "protective best friend" thing? Do you need me to assure you I'm not going to hurt Poppy?'

'That would be good,' Eleanor agreed with an

overly sweet smile as a palace staffer appeared with a trolley of drinks and food.

'Ellie,' Poppy interjected, but again, Adrastos spoke sooner, once they were alone.

'I have no intention of hurting Poppy.'

'I suppose that's something.'

'What more would you like, little sister?'

'I want to understand how two people who almost seem to have made an art form of *avoiding* one another have decided to date.'

'People grow and change,' Poppy said carefully. 'We're just dating. It's not serious.'

'It's serious,' Eleanor disagreed. 'When you both come and stay here. When you go out on dates looking like this.' Ellie gestured to Poppy.

'What do I look like?'

'Beautiful, of course,' Eleanor supplied quickly. 'But you also look…'

'Yes?' Adrastos's voice held more than a hint of warning.

'Like you're being groomed for a specific role.'

Poppy's eyes widened. 'What do you mean?'

'You look like a princess-in-waiting, Pops. I know you might not be taking this seriously yet, but you should be aware that everyone else will be.'

'Everyone else will have to wait for an official

announcement before they start ordering their wedding attire,' Adrastos said quietly.

Poppy wanted to shake him. There was no 'waiting for an announcement'. There would be no announcement, no wedding.

'Maybe she's right.' Poppy turned in the seat, so she was facing only Adrastos, and suddenly it was just the two of them in the room. She lifted a hand to his chest, pressing it there, fingers splayed wide, mind racing. 'Maybe this is too public. Too much, too soon.'

'It's not.'

'But what if it is?'

He pressed a hand over hers and moved his face closer to hers. 'Because I've anticipated that. There will be very little press intrusion into our night, Poppy. You must relax.'

But how could she? Everything seemed to be spinning completely out of control. As if he understood that she was on the precipice of a panic attack, he leaned forward and kissed her slowly, gently, keeping her hand between them, his own hand stroking hers, just as his mouth moved over hers. 'Relax,' he murmured, and she pulled back a little, somehow dredging up a smile, and it was not a smile for Eleanor's benefit, but one that came to her naturally.

'Okay.' She realised Ellie wasn't the only Aetos she trusted. He reached across and took the champagne flute from her spare hand, placing it on his side table, then turned to face his sister. Eleanor was watching them with unashamed interest.

'We're going to leave now, Eleanor.'

The Princess was very still for a moment and then finally nodded. 'I can see that.'

Poppy wondered at the tone in her best friend's voice. There was something there she didn't like. Sadness?

'Do you want to come with us?' Poppy heard herself offer, so the hand of Adrastos's that was holding hers squeezed a little tighter.

Eleanor laughed and shook her head, suddenly herself again. 'I can just imagine how my big brother would enjoy that. No, thank you. I'll be your third wheel another time. Go, have fun.' She turned to Adrastos. 'Take care of her.'

'I intend to.'

CHAPTER EIGHT

THE CAR PULLED out from the palace and, as expected, flashbulbs erupted. Despite his having made the arrangements to assure the utmost secrecy, the palace was being watched even more closely than normal in light of the 'news' of Adrastos's latest fling. Of their own volition, his eyes slid across to Poppy, in the seat beside him, her lips compressed, her hands clasped tight in her lap.

'This is not supposed to feel like torture.'

'It doesn't,' she reacted quickly, apology in the little grimace she offered him. 'It's just…a little overwhelming.'

His hands tightened on the wheel.

Of course it would seem overwhelming to Poppy. She had no experience with dating anyone, let alone someone who brought this level of scrutiny. In the rear-vision mirror, he saw a motorbike give chase and expelled a rough sound of impatience, then quickly muted it when he noticed Poppy's flinch.

'You get used to it.' It was a throwaway comment he immediately regretted, because it somehow implied he wanted *her* to get used to it, which might almost suggest he wanted her to stick around, beyond the terms of their fake relationship, and of course he didn't. Adrastos couldn't wait to get through this and find a satisfying way to 'end it' for his family's benefit, so he could get back to his real life.

And go back to only seeing Poppy a couple of times a year, he tacked on mentally, for good measure, the vow an important one to make to himself.

Poppy turned in the seat, angling to face him, and all he could focus on was her slender thighs, exposed by the way her dress had crept up as she'd taken her seat. 'Do you?'

Her eyes pinned him in place earnestly. He forced himself to keep his attention on the road. 'Eventually.' The word was given as a grudging concession to the fact it had taken him quite some time to accept this level of scrutiny. And he certainly didn't enjoy it.

'Do you mind?'

'I accept it comes with the position.'

She frowned. 'But you don't like it?'

'Who would like it?' He responded quickly, turning the car down a side street, away from the embassies that were in the suburbs closest to the palace, leading them to a fashionable precinct with streets of restaurants.

'Lots of people, I suppose,' she said with a lift of those incredible shoulders. He really should have used a chauffeur but, for some reason, he'd railed against that. With Poppy, he wanted to be completely in charge. He wanted to call the shots, to run the show. He wanted to be answerable for everything that happened between them. Besides, it was harder to speak frankly with the presence of staff, and he liked being honest and open with her. As she was basically a member of his family, he could trust her implicitly. 'Celebrity has become a level of attainment in and of itself.'

He grunted his agreement with that, but it was something Adrastos had never personally felt. 'There are many good things about the position of privilege I occupy. Having my every waking move dissected by the press is not one of them.'

'Of course not.'

'You must have experienced this with Eleanor.'

'It's different. She isn't followed like you are.'

'For that, I am supremely grateful.'

'She lives a mostly normal life,' Poppy continued thoughtfully. 'I mean, there are photographers. There's interest in her, of course. She's adored. And reported on. But not to this extent.

When we were at university, we were just like any other eighteen-year-olds.'

'I'm sure there are a great many secrets you could tell me about my sister,' he said, surprising them both with a grin.

Poppy blinked, a study in wide-eyed innocence. 'You must know I could never tell you anything that Ellie had told me in confidence.'

The fact she thought he'd even ask was one of the strongest indictments of his character he'd ever known. He focussed on the road. 'I would never ask you to.'

She breathed out. 'Sorry. I'm nervous.'

'You don't have to be. I'm not really a big bad wolf.'

'Aren't you?' she asked, then pressed a hand to her lips. 'I'm sorry again. That just came out. Sometimes, when I'm with you, I find it just far too easy to say the wrong thing.'

'Why is it the wrong thing, if it's what you really think?'

'Well, we can have many thoughts,' she said after a beat. 'But not all of them reflect how we truly feel.'

'A fascinating comment, Poppy. I'm tempted to analyse that further and ask how you really feel about me.'

He turned to face her, but Poppy had grown pale. He was pushing her too far, teasing her.

Reaching out, he curved his fingers over her knee and she startled. Yes, he was glad no chauffeur was around to witness this.

'Hey.' If they weren't being followed by a pesky photographer on a bike, he'd have been tempted to pull over and kiss all these nerves away. 'I promise, this is going to be fun. I know this isn't real, but, for tonight, let's pretend we're actually dating. I think we could both enjoy that, hmm?'

That was the problem! If Poppy wasn't very, very careful, the lines between reality and make-believe would get woefully blurred and she'd wake up half in danger of believing that Adrastos actually cared for her.

With a heart rate that wouldn't slow, she waited as Adrastos pulled the car into the sweeping drive of a five-star hotel in the city centre. She'd heard of it, but never been.

'A hotel?'

'The bar,' he said with a nod. 'Come with me.' He stepped out of his side of the car at the same time a hotel valet opened the door to hers. It was only as she exited that Poppy became aware of the security presence—four men emerging from a car behind them—and then, several motorbikes with paparazzi. But Adrastos was right there, a reassuring arm around her waist drawing her close to his side so she forgot about everything and everyone and was conscious only of how well she fitted against him, of how warm and masculine he was, how hard and strong. His arm was like a clamp, his body a brick wall, and she was water, melting and liquid, filling in the gaps.

Once they stepped into the foyer, the paparazzi disappeared—no one followed them inside except for his security guards, who travelled up in the lift with them. Even then, Poppy was barely aware of their presence, because once inside the lift Adrastos seemed so much bigger and stronger, his body wrapping around her, if not physically, at least in terms of presence.

The doors pinged open and the security guards stepped out, two on either side, forming a passage for them to exit. But instead of leaving, Adrastos turned his body, shielding Poppy from the view of the bar.

'Adrastos?' She blinked up at him, her mouth as dry as the desert. He was looking at her in a way that was now familiar to Poppy. She bit down on her lip, blinking up at him. 'You're going to kiss me again, aren't you?'

'Yes.'

'Why?'

'You look to need it.'

'I'm not sure if that's true.'

'But, Poppy, haven't we established I'm the expert on all things kissing?'

She rolled her eyes. 'You know, your ego is—' She didn't get a chance to finish the sentence. He kissed her and she smiled, because he was right. She had needed it, and being kissed by him like this, being held by him, was enough to burn her soul to the ground in the best possible way.

The bar was so super exclusive that paparazzi access was forbidden, and the clientele was high-profile enough to assure a degree of anonymity. Though, no, Poppy reflected, leaning back in their booth seat. Anonymity was not quite the right word. Adrastos could never truly be anonymous. He was recognisable to anyone in the world who didn't live under a rock, and even here, in a bar crammed full of billionaires, celebrities and nobility, there was Adrastos, a wholly different species.

Poppy tried not to focus on how many women ogled him.

Nor to think about how many of these women he'd ogled back. Or more.

But it was impossible to blot those thoughts, impossible not to reflect on how active his love life had been, nor to think about how active it would be again after this.

So even though they sat in a private booth

with exquisite views over the city, and Adrastos did an excellent job of acting as though she were the only woman in the entire world, Poppy couldn't help folding a little in on herself as the night went on.

He ordered a beer and she a champagne, and her nerves eased slightly, but it just took the passing by of one glamorous woman for Poppy to be reminded of the fact she didn't belong here. She wasn't a part of Adrastos's world.

'Tell me about your work,' he commanded, fingers trailing her shoulder then drawing circles, reminding her of the way he'd eased her to sleep the night before. She shivered, a tingle of pleasure, of warmth and awareness, then cleared her throat, trying to focus.

'My work can be a depressing topic.'

He dipped his head. 'Yet you do it anyway.'

'Someone's got to.'

'Why you?'

'You think I should be doing something else?'

He narrowed his gaze. 'I didn't say that.'

'I always wanted to practise law. I wasn't sure until I started studying what I'd specialise in, but the truth is human rights are so important and as we make our way through the twenty-first century, I'm shocked by the erosion of rights in so many parts of the world. It makes my skin crawl to think how some people live.'

'So you're driven by a desire to fix the world?' he asked, voice light, even when his eyes were stripping away her layers, peeling right into the centre of her being.

'It's sure not the salary,' she said with a wry grimace.

He lifted a brow.

'I'm employed by a not-for-profit organisation. If I was looking to make my fortune, I'd have gone into commercial litigation, but working for oligarchs who want to make themselves richer by selling boats to other billionaires isn't how I see myself spending my days.'

'And you work long hours,' he said, neatly bringing the conversation back to what she suspected he really wanted to discuss—her lack of a sex life.

She sipped her champagne. 'Yes.' She did. Not because she always had to, but because it was one way to avoid entanglements. 'I like to be good at what I do.'

'Why do I suspect you're excellent at it?'

Her eyes widened. 'I don't know,' she said with a shake of her head.

'Poppy?'

She stared at him; she was drowning.

'There must be a reason,' he said after a beat, his meaning clear despite the apparent change of subject. 'Someone broke your heart?'

She took another sip of her champagne, almost choking. 'No. Never. Really, I'm very boring, Adrastos.'

He bit back whatever he'd been about to say. 'That's not how I would describe you.'

Beneath the table, she pressed a hand to his thigh. 'Really, you don't have to do this.'

'Do what?'

'Flatter me.' She blinked away from him, chagrined by this conversation. '*Pretend*, when it's just the two of us.'

'Didn't we agree we'd both pretend tonight?'

'Yes, but the flattery, it's just not necessary. I know the kind of women you're usually with. I know I'm not like them.'

His eyes skimmed her face. 'You're interested in the women I date?'

She rolled her eyes and hoped her demurral would sound convincing. 'No.' She ignored his sceptical look. 'I just mean I've seen stuff. Stories. Over the years. I know you date a certain type of woman, and I'm not it.'

'In what way?'

She shook her head. 'We shouldn't do this.'

'Why not? I'm interested in what you think of my love life.'

'Well, for a start, I wouldn't call it a love life so much as a sex life,' she responded quickly, then wished she hadn't when she felt him pull back a little.

'Don't stop,' he said, reaching for his beer and having a drink.

His eyes narrowed, and he moved closer, so their bodies were touching beneath the table and Poppy was grateful for the linen cloth, because if any guest did decide to take a photo with their phone, the image would be every bit as intimate as the photos taken on the night of her birthday, if not more so.

'Not that I give this matter much thought,' she said a little unevenly, her body surging with attraction so she was far too aware of him on a cellular level to think clearly.

'Too busy saving the world?'

'Something like that,' she lied. Of course she'd thought about his hectic sex life—how could she not, when she knew it was a source of pain for Eleanor and Clementine? Loyalty had made her cross with Adrastos. She went to pull her legs away from him, but beneath the table, his hand curved over her thigh, holding her still.

'Why did you want to sleep with me?'

The question caught something in Poppy's throat. Her eyes flew to Adrastos's and she tried desperately to think of an answer.

'Don't lie to me,' he said quietly. 'I want to understand.'

She opened her mouth then slammed it shut. She supposed it wasn't an unreasonable question. After all, she'd somewhat blindsided him with her virginity. 'I didn't plan for that to happen,' she muttered.

'No, but once it did, you could have pulled back.'

'You were there. You know how you made me feel.'

'You let me kiss you, when no other man has come close.'

Poppy hadn't intended to talk to Adrastos about this, but sitting so close, touching beneath the table, she was hypnotised by him, just as always.

'I've thought about that, over the years,' she said, softly, her lashes dark fans against her soft, milky skin, her attention focussed on the past so she didn't notice the intensity of Adrastos's stare. 'I mean, I'm so out of step.' She shrugged self-consciously. 'Ellie, our other friends, they all went through the normal teenage stuff, and I just...didn't. I never had a crush,' she said breathlessly, ignoring the feeling beneath her ribs, the heat emanating from Adrastos, the pulsing in the back of her brain making her wonder if maybe that wasn't true, if maybe she'd had a crush on him all along. She pushed the thought aside because it was too difficult to contemplate and things between them were complicated enough. 'I knew I wanted to study law. I needed good grades, so I studied hard.' Her eyes moved to Adrastos thoughtfully. 'My parents praised me for my grades, you know. They were so proud of me; I didn't want to let them down. It's silly, isn't it? I mean, they aren't here any more, but I still felt—'

'It's not silly,' he demurred. 'Not to me.'

Her eyes met his and something strange crackled in the air between them. Was he quick to agree because of his own feelings of loss and grief?

'But it was more than just being studious.' She inhaled softly, tried to find the words for her thoughts, then shook her head. 'You're going to think it's childish.'

'Try me.'

'Well, I was fourteen when they—when I lost them—and my view of their relationship, of all relationships, is I suppose a little stuck in time. When they died, I saw them as these most perfect people, as a perfect couple. They were so happy, so in love. I'm sure that there were times they argued, that there was more nuance to their relationship. As I've got older, I've learned that all relationships take work, that people can't always be perfect and happy and life isn't completely rosy. But what I saw then? It was like a fairy tale.' She sighed again. 'And I guess, somewhere in the back of my mind, I unconsciously decided that that's what all relationships *should* be like.' She lifted her shoulders. 'That if you can't love someone as my parents loved each other, what's the point?'

He frowned, but at least he didn't criticise that thought, nor did he argue with her.

'I imagine your parents didn't love each other like that right from the start,' he pointed out after a brief, thoughtful pause. 'That kind of connection grows with time. Did it occur to you that in order to share that love, you'd need to start with a date? A friendship that will grow over weeks and months?'

'Speaking from experience?' She couldn't help probing.

His smile was tight, almost dismissive. 'We're talking about you right now.'

She lifted her eyes to his and blinked away, almost too embarrassed to say anything else. But having started down the path of baring her soul, she wasn't inclined now to stop. 'It's more than just wanting a perfect relationship,' she said, pulling her lips to the side, lost in thought. 'There's also a question of...chemistry.'

He lifted a brow.

'You know, I guess I just haven't felt it that

often.' She didn't want to admit she'd never felt it with anyone but him. 'Even as a teenager.'

Perhaps he had questions. In fact, she was sure he did. But Adrastos, always in control, bided his time. 'That sounds like the opposite of my teen-age experience,' he said with a half-grimace, so she couldn't help responding with a smile.

'When hormones ruled your every move?'

'I would like to think I still showed them who was boss, but that would be a lie,' he said with a shake of his head. 'I think I could have found chemistry with a lamp post…'

She laughed, even as a warning bell sounded in her mind. His words reinforced why she had to keep her focus about this, why she had to re-member that, for Adrastos, she was just like any other woman.

And for you? a voice in her head demanded, even as Poppy shied away from answering the question.

'I'm curious, though, Poppy,' he said, leaning closer and almost kissing the words against the flesh just beneath her ear. It was so sensitive, she trembled. 'You still haven't answered my question. Why did you decide to sleep with me?'

Her eyes flared wide and her heart twisted in on itself. 'I—' She bit down on her lower lip. 'Wanted to,' she said, after a beat.

'To lose your virginity,' he murmured, lifting

his head just far enough so their eyes could meet. 'And you thought someone like me, someone who sees sex as an inconsequential act, would be the easiest solution?'

It wasn't accurate, not really. She hadn't expected that night to mean anything to him, but that wasn't why she'd chosen Adrastos, and having him believe that sat strangely in her gut. And yet, she didn't correct him. Some ancient self-preservation technique had her shrugging, almost as if in agreement.

'I don't know if I really thought it through,' she said, finally, brushing the subject away with an overbright smile. 'It happened and, unlike you, I don't regret it.'

CHAPTER NINE

BUT HE DIDN'T regret it either. He could think something was a mistake without wishing it hadn't happened. It was a technicality, but an important one, and yet Adrastos didn't correct Poppy. As with all things Poppy, her answers had only given him more questions, but he was in no rush to push the subject tonight. Again he thought of an animal in the forest, of not wanting to frighten her into bolting.

There was something about her, a fragility that was almost at odds with her success as a lawyer and her outward confidence.

When she was fourteen, he'd wanted to protect her, and those instincts were still a part of him. It was why he'd gone with her at the party when she'd approached him. He hadn't known then that she was about to proposition him, but he'd seen urgency in her eyes, and recognised that she was coming to him, just to him, that she needed him.

And why had he slept with her? He wondered,

as he showered that night, lathering his body until it was covered in white suds then standing beneath the stream of water until his hair was plastered over his brow. He was no virgin, but a man with more than enough experience under his belt to control his libido—or so he'd thought.

Frustration twisted in his gut.

He felt like a stranger to himself.

Where usually Adrastos could understand his own motives, his reasons for acting, in this regard, he drew a blank. After all, he'd leapt at the chance to take her to bed. Whether she was a virgin or not was beside the point. Sex with Poppy was still…layered. Complicated. Made so by her relationships with his family, her place *within* his family.

He groaned, pressing his head forward, against the tiles. The water was so loud in his ears—or was that his own pulse?—that at first he didn't hear the knocking on the door, but it grew louder, and he switched the water off impatiently.

'Yes?'

'Are you okay, Adrastos?'

His body responded instantly. Naked and wet, his groin tightened at the sound of Poppy's voice, and his heart thudded heavily against his ribs.

'Why?'

'You've…um…been in there a while, and you just groaned as though you'd stubbed your toe.'

He couldn't help smiling, but it was a smile of irritation and impatience. Whatever desire had flooded his body and thrown rational thought away on the night of Poppy's party, it was still a part of him, dictating and controlling him, so before he could think it through he switched the water back on and turned towards the door.

'If you are concerned about my welfare, you are very welcome to come in and check on me.'

Having thrown down the challenge, he had no real expectation of her taking it up. Poppy had very wisely put a stop to things whenever he'd kissed her, but he stood still, waiting, for several long, tense seconds, hope swelling in his chest until he realised that of *course* she wasn't going to walk into the bathroom as he showered. He reached behind his back for the tap just as the door creaked open and her familiar, beautiful face peeped around the door.

Not her body, which she kept firmly anchored on the other side, as though she were afraid of stepping into the abyss. But her face was enough. Her eyes, huge and round, stared at him, locked to his at first, before dropping to his lips, which she hungrily studied, then falling lower, flashing, almost, to his cock, lingering there, so he grew hard and hungry beneath her inspection, then lower again, sweeping over his legs until she closed her eyes and stayed right where she was, head peering around the crack in the door, elegant neck aching to be touched.

He groaned at the futility of this, of the frustration. 'Well?' His voice, though, was pleasingly level. 'Are you going to come in, *deliciae*?'

Her eyes flared open, locking to his once more, and he felt her indecision and uncertainty like a sledgehammer. A curse filled his mind, reverberated around his skull, as he contemplated his next move. Only Adrastos wasn't sure that this was a time for thinking.

With Poppy, he didn't think. And maybe that was just how it had to be between the two of them? Instincts alone had brought them together—his, on the night of her twenty-first, then hers three years later. And his when he'd thrown caution to the wind and ignored what he *should* have done, what he'd known was right, and done what he'd simply, desperately wanted. Poppy's when she'd concocted this plan to save hurting his family's feelings or making things difficult for Adrastos.

Their instincts had guided them and maybe their lot in life was to act first, regret later, but he couldn't be sure.

Out of nowhere, he remembered what she'd

said only hours earlier: *'Unlike you, I don't regret it.'*

Moving without thinking, he stepped from the shower, and Poppy stayed where she was, just a head, until he opened the bathroom door wider, eyes probing, challenging, warning her to stop him now if she wanted to.

But to his delight and relief, once the door was open, and their bodies close, it was Poppy who moved first, melding to him as she pushed up onto the tips of her toes and tilted her head back so they could kiss. He was naked and wet and she fitted against him so perfectly, her body so soft and sweet, reminding him of something he'd felt the first night they'd kissed, years earlier.

There had been so much passion in that kiss but there had also been a strange, eerie sort of peace, like the stars in the desert sky in the very middle of the night. Clarity. Ancient wisdom. He'd felt as though he was every single version of himself that he was ever destined to be, distilled into one omniscient moment.

A strange way to feel as he'd simultaneously delighted in the mastery of his body over another's, but that was the effect Poppy had had on him, and he felt it again now. He was conscious of nothing. Not the still-running water behind them, not the loud pounding of his heart, not the ticking of the clock in his suite, not the palace, not his family, nothing.

'I have wanted to do that all night,' she said, pulling back a little and blinking up at him, surprised by the admission, or perhaps by the passion that had ignited the second they'd touched. But Adrastos couldn't bear the thought of Poppy pulling away from him again. He couldn't kiss her and catch fire and not give into it.

'I kissed you earlier.'

'But there were people everywhere,' she replied breathlessly. 'Watching. Possibly recording...'

He should have been glad for her awareness of that because Adrastos, despite his years of living in the public eye, hadn't had the fortitude to think of their surrounds for even a moment.

'I want you,' he said, rather than analyse why he'd been incapable of being more discreet.

Her eyes were shuttered from him then, hiding whatever she was feeling, and her skin went from flushed to pale, so he had no idea what he'd said or done to make her prevaricate, but he felt her uncertainty suddenly and wanted to release a deep, guttural growl.

'Poppy, listen to me.' He caught her face in his hands, held it steady, stared deep into her eyes. 'You have no experience with men. I don't know why you doubt the truth of my words, why you think I would say I want you if I didn't, but please stop. I want *you*. Here and now, I ache for you in a way I will never be able to put into words.'

Her lips parted and something shifted in her features. Confusion, wonderment, and something else. Uncertainty? But it was gone, in an instant. She smiled at him, a bright smile that he wasn't sure he'd ever seen on her face, certainly not directed at him, and then lifted her brows. 'Well, then, Your Highness, what exactly are you waiting for?'

He growled as he swept down and picked her up, carrying her against his wet frame, right back into the shower—more than big enough to comfortably accommodate the two of them—and kissing her hungrily as he stripped her out of her beautiful dress, growing darker and wetter by the minute as the shower drenched it.

It was harder to strip from her body than it should have been. The fabric clung to her wet skin, and he felt utterly thwarted and quite mad with longing by the time it finally dropped to the tiles beneath them and she stepped out of it, revealing a simple pair of briefs and a strapless bra.

Such utilitarian underwear, really, as though she'd chosen it with no thought of him seeing it, and yet it was somehow the sexiest fabric he'd ever seen. Nonetheless, he discarded it quickly too, seeking her nakedness, needing her to be as bare-skinned as he was.

The first time they'd made love had been her first time ever, and Adrastos hadn't even found his own release. That was something he intended to rectify. In fact, there was much he wanted to change about what that experience had been.

Poppy had deserved so much more than that for her first time, he realised with a growing sense of anger. How had she ever thought a one-night stand would be enough? She deserved to have been seduced properly, kissed until she was mindless, built to a fever state then made love to again and again until her body was so awash with sensations that she could barely stand.

Suddenly, he saw the gift she'd given him, the responsibility, and wanted to live up to it. He wanted to be not just her first but her best, for ever, so that no man who came after him in her life could ever equal the pleasure Adrastos had given her.

The thought evoked something strange and primal in his chest, a feeling that stirred almost barbaric instincts to life. It was normal to feel jealous, imagining other men with your lover. At least, he imagined it was: Adrastos had never been a particularly jealous man.

He didn't want to think about Poppy's next lover or lovers.

With a dark sound deep in his throat, he kissed her harder, more hungrily, as he lifted her and pressed her slim body against the tiles, standing between her hips, holding her easily at his waist, his arousal hard and throbbing for her, so he was almost mindless with desire. Wet and slippery made this somehow more hedonistic and elemental.

He moved his mouth to her breasts, revelling in the feel of them in his palms, his mouth, his stubbled jaw dragging across them until he knew every inch of her. The sounds she made, her little cries, were driving him wild, making it almost impossible to resist driving into her then and there.

But Adrastos wanted to slow this down, to make it last. He wanted to make this a night to remember. He wanted to give Poppy the sort of pleasure she should have understood by now, to show her everything her body could sense and feel. He wanted…everything.

With a guttural noise of impatience, he knelt down, hands on her hips pinning her to the wall as he pressed his mouth to her sex, tasting, teasing, listening to her cries of pleasure, feeling the wobble in her legs as she struggled to support herself and, finally, her shuddering release as she moaned his name over and over. Water doused him, doused them, but nothing could wash away his intensely urgent need for her. As he stood, their eyes met and the air between them seemed to light up with sparks, her mouth was parted and her gaze seemed to be pleading with him in some way.

He understood, without words. Her fear, her surprise, her desire to feel *more*. He snapped off the water and grabbed Poppy in one motion, lifting her against his chest, pausing only briefly to grab a huge black towel from the rack. At the foot of his bed, he placed Poppy down and dried her, but even that was a temptation and torment. She was so beautiful. He shifted his gaze to her face, staring at her, and something shifted in his gut, or his chest, or his throat, making it harder to breathe, to think, for his heart to pump blood through his body.

'You turned into a woman overnight.'

Her smile was slow, and wry. 'Not quite overnight. You just missed a lot of time here.'

He had. He'd been busy for a long time. Busy with the military, in which he held several command positions, busy with policy work for the government committees he served on. Busy staying away? From his family, from their expectations, from Nicholas's absence. From Poppy, too?

He kissed her rather than dwell on that: why should he want to avoid Poppy? She spent so much time with Eleanor, it wasn't as though her presence in the palace was a problem for him. Particularly not when she made his parents so happy.

'I noticed at your twenty-first,' he admitted. 'I came home and, all of a sudden, you were all grown up, and so very, very tempting.'

Her eyes closed and he had a familiar sense, a misgiving; she'd reacted like that before, to something else he'd said, only he couldn't quite remember. It was as if she didn't want to hear the compliment, or didn't believe it.

'Stop talking,' she said with a rueful shake of her head, an attempt at a joke, and he let it go, because it suited him fine not to talk. Adrastos wasn't one for conversing while making love. Not usually, anyway. He'd never bought into the 'spending the night' concept either. For him, it was sex, and that was that.

Better to avoid entanglements, raised hopes, better to leave before anyone could ask him to stay.

'Your wish is my command.'

'Isn't it meant to be the other way around?'

'We can take turns.'

'I like the sound of that. Only…' Her lips pulled to the side. 'I don't really know what to do.'

He moved closer, so close that his mouth brushed hers as he spoke. 'You're already doing it.' And then, he pulled her with him back to the bed, his body so hard, his need so great, he couldn't think straight, he couldn't do anything except allow his body the freedom to touch every inch of her, to be in this moment feeling, pleasuring, giving, receiving…

Poppy felt different the next morning. Physically different. She was stretched and sore and her nerves buzzed and hummed with new pleasures rendered and experienced, with the feeling that Adrastos had made her his so utterly and completely she wasn't sure how she'd ever think of herself as her own person again.

That thought had her sitting upright, her face draining of colour, and her eyes seeking him on the other side of the bed. She was relieved that he wasn't there, even when her heart gave a funny little clutch and her lips tugged downwards. But the truth was, seeing Adrastos now would be too much.

She needed time and space to give some perspective to what they'd shared.

Or, she thought, her frown deepening, she needed to talk to someone, to her very best friend in the whole world, who always helped Poppy know what she wanted when Poppy was lost. But how could Poppy turn to Eleanor at a time like this? What would she say?

She dismissed the idea completely.

This was her ruse, and the last thing she wanted was to involved Ellie in any of it.

But that strange sense of doom, of danger, lurked on the edge of Poppy's mind. She felt as though she were walking through a field of snakes, burrowed deep in their holes but likely to emerge at any point and strike. She felt danger prodding her and yet she couldn't explain it.

This was temporary. They both knew what this was: a pretend relationship. The sex was by the by. Poppy was attracted to Adrastos. It was clear Adrastos felt the same, but Poppy wasn't naïve enough to think that she was special to him in any way. If Poppy hadn't been here, Adrastos would have found another woman to be with. That was who he was. It was who he'd always be.

She shook her head, wondering why that knowledge, a piece of certainty she'd held for a long time, suddenly made her throat feel as though it were filled with sharp rocks. Why should she care that Adrastos was a serial bed-hopper?

It wasn't her business.

And this was just sex.

Her heart gave that strange twist again and she dropped her head forward, staring at the crisp white coverlet of his bed. Where was he? Poppy told herself again that she was glad he wasn't here, but, deep down, Adrastos might have been the only person on the face of the earth who could have helped calm her fluttering nerves—by kissing them right out of her head—and he was nowhere to be seen.

He hadn't intentionally avoided her, and yet giving both of them space had seemed wise after last night. He couldn't think of it without a growing sense of disquiet. It hadn't been 'just sex', for the pure reason, he reassured himself, that neither of them had been able to leave again afterwards. Sharing a bed, naked, limbs entwined, they'd fallen asleep with Poppy's head on his chest, his hand curved around her back, fingers possessively splayed over her hip, and when he'd woken several hours later, it had been because Poppy was kissing his chest, still half asleep, in the early hours of the morning. He suspected she hadn't even been aware of what she was doing, but Adrastos had kissed her back, waking her up the rest of the way, until they'd come together in a frantic, desperate joining, as if neither had known the other's body for years, not hours.

He'd been too wired to go back to sleep after that. He'd waited for Poppy to slip into dreams, then pushed back the covers and strode out of the room, pausing only to grab some clothes on his way to his office, where he greeted the dawn, staring out at the forest, admiring it for its ancient trees and wisdom, for the fierce danger that lurked beneath the beautiful, almost serene-seeming surface.

It was the kind of forest that made up postcards of this region, so picturesque and pretty, but there were many threats amongst those broad, round trunks. Predators, the weather, the lack of cell service so if you didn't know exactly what you were doing and became lost, there was no easy rescue. Adrastos had been told, as a young boy, never to go into the forest alone, which of course had only made him determined to do exactly that. But he was no fool: he understood the dangers and so he respected them. He took precautions each time, testing his strength as one grew and developed a muscle, until he was confident he could walk amongst those trees like any of the predators who owned the woods.

Just as he was confident he could control what was happening with Poppy. True, it was different from his usual relationships, for many reasons, not least because he knew her and, worse, she knew him. Really knew him—in the way you couldn't avoid having knowledge of a person when you'd been in their home and immersed in their family. She saw facets of him he liked to keep all to himself.

But that was also to his advantage, because she understood what he was like. She'd seen his attitude to relationships, she'd heard his parents and sister bemoan his inability to settle down, she knew that after their very gentle, respectful 'break-up', he'd go back to his normal life, and she'd go back to hers, and they'd return to seeing each other a few times a year, when palace life brought them home at the same time.

It was a thought he held like a talisman, but, much like his early walks into the forest, he sensed danger in the idea, because he was no fool. Sleeping with Poppy was different and new, and he would need to train himself to treat her like any of his other lovers; he'd need a different kind of strength to simply walk away from her and stay away.

Adrastos, fortunately, never failed once he'd set his mind to something and, in this, he was determined.

CHAPTER TEN

SHE FELT INEXPLICABLY SHY! Poppy knew these people, loved them, and yet sitting at the table, beside Adrastos, she found her tongue was tied in knots and her fingers quivering so she had to hold them in her lap. She was nervous and overcome, a jangle of feelings, of awareness. She felt, she realised, as the waiters brought out plates ladened with local delicacies, as though she were on a first date. With Adrastos, and his whole family.

She could barely look at the man, for goodness' sake! After the intimacy of the night before, after the way he'd made her feel, after the way *he'd* felt, she reminded herself with a deep crimson blush spreading over her cheeks, she was unprepared for how to go from that level of sensual connection to this, to normal life, to pretending they were just themselves, and yet not themselves, because Poppy and Adrastos had never been *this*. A couple. A pretend couple.

She sipped her water, barely listening to the

conversation swirling around her, barely conscious of anything, except at one point, when Adrastos physically stiffened beside her, so that his tension was impossible to ignore. Poppy sat up straighter and tuned into what was being said.

The King was speaking—with obvious pride—shaking his head at how naturally Adrastos had handled a trade negotiation. 'They can be difficult to work with, you know. I've never found it easy, at least. But you, of course, had them eating out of the palm of your hand. You will have to teach me how you did that.' Alexander's eyes crinkled at the corners and Clementine added some noises of congratulation. Adrastos's face was ash beneath his tanned complexion, and when he thanked them, it was in a voice that was almost completely devoid of emotion.

Poppy skimmed his face, trying to understand, but then he turned to Poppy and her pulse almost throttled her, and her body flooded with warmth and need and all thoughts of understanding Adrastos fled from her mind.

The festive season in the palace was beautiful and wondrous and usually Poppy adored it, but she found it hard to focus on the little traditions this year, on enjoying the quintessentially local food. In fact, she could barely taste anything!

Somehow, she made it through the main course, and then dessert, but afterwards, when

Clementine suggested they adjourn to the drawing room, where the family traditionally listened to classical music and drank something very similar to gin but made from berries grown only in Stomland, Poppy made her excuses.

'I have a bit of a headache,' she murmured apologetically excusing herself, barely able to meet anyone's eyes, least of all Adrastos's. Would he be annoyed with her? Or secretly relieved if she left, so he could also stop pretending?

'I'll come with you.' His voice was low, gruff.

'Oh, no, no,' she said, far too quickly, and had to force a smile to avoid arousing suspicion. 'That's not necessary,' she added with a lift of her shoulders. 'I'll be okay. I just need an early night.' She turned back to the King and Queen, curtseying without thinking about it—a small gesture that was always observed, regardless of how close they were.

'Are you sure you're okay?' Ellie asked. 'You look pale.'

'I'm fine,' she stressed, reaching out and squeezing her friend's hand, but not before the sting of tears threatened at the backs of her eyes. She couldn't bear the solicitous enquiry. Not when she was lying her butt off to these people, her makeshift family.

It wasn't the lie though, she realised, when

she was safely back in Adrastos's suite, having a cup of tea on the balcony, wrapped up in a thick, woollen blanket. It was the intimacy they'd shared last night. Not sex. Intimacy. True, life-changing closeness and connection. It was more than just physical desire. Somehow, being with him like that had kickstarted a response inside Poppy that had intensified as the day went on. It was as if he'd become a part of her soul, and with every breath his hold on her spread, until he became all she could think about.

'How are you feeling?'

She should have expected his return—surely she didn't think he'd just let her run away to his room with the complaint of a headache and not come to check on her? And yet surprise was on her features when, not fifteen minutes later, Adrastos stepped onto the balcony and frowned, because snow was in the air and Poppy had chosen here, of all places, to drink tea?

'Fine.' But her smile was stretched and her gaze frustratingly skittish, just as it had been over dinner, so he wanted to kiss her more than ever. It seemed to be the simplest way to make her relax, to simply exist and not overthink, to bring her back into the light, but it was also a way of delaying, of running, and Adrastos had never tolerated cowardice.

'No headache?'

She pulled a face. 'Brain ache, more like.'

'Explain.' He crossed his arms over his chest, mainly to stop himself from reaching for her, from bringing her to stand against his chest. He wanted to comfort her, but something held him back, something vital that he didn't fully comprehend, yet respected nonetheless.

'I just hate lying to them.' She wrinkled her nose and lifted a hand as if to forestall his possible response to that. 'I know, I know. It was all my idea. My stupid, stupid idea.'

His nostrils flared with the force of his sigh. '*Deliciae*, as you pointed out, we had very limited options once those photos were printed.'

'Yes, but I know you would have just faced the music without flinching.'

'Far less frightening for me to do so.'

She blinked up at him.

'They're my family,' he said, gently, crouching down then, ignoring his better instincts and putting a hand on her knee. 'And while I know they love you as if you were their biological child, it's understandable that you would feel less secure in that love. You didn't want to lose them, as you lost your own parents, and so you did the one thing you could think of to make that unlikely.'

A tear rolled down her cheek and he bit back a curse.

'You will never lose them, Poppy. Our stupidity on that night aside, you are their daughter.'

She shook her head, as if to clear his words from the sky.

'It's untenable,' she whispered. 'After this is over, how do we go back?' Huge, haunted eyes looked at him, but she wasn't really looking at Adrastos, so much as desperately hoping to find strength in his frame, a strength he wasn't sure he could give but knew she needed.

So he forced himself to convey it, to show absolute certainty even when he didn't completely feel it. 'We simply go back,' he said with a shrug. 'It's not complicated.'

Her eyes skimmed his face thoughtfully, as though she was analysing that from every angle. 'I want to believe that.'

'You have no experience,' he reminded her.

'But you do.'

He dipped his head, not wanting to think about former lovers. For the first time in his life, he felt an unusual sense of remorse, a wish that he'd known fewer women, a wish to erase them from his memories so there was room only for Poppy.

'So this is normal,' she said with a slow shift of her head. 'You can turn this on and off, like a tap?'

The directness of her question caught him off guard. It wasn't accurate at all. 'It's more that I can enjoy an experience for what it is, be grateful for it, and then move on,' he said after a moment, glad that his voice sounded so measured and reasonable. 'I am grateful for this experience with you, Poppy, even though it is far more complication than I would usually entertain in my personal life.'

'Why?' she asked, eyes locked to his as she sipped her tea. All night at dinner, she'd avoided looking at him, so he'd wanted to reach out and draw her chin towards him, to force their eyes to meet, so he could understand why she was so quiet. But now, in the delicate silver of the moonlight, she wouldn't stop looking at him, so he felt almost too seen, far too visible.

'Do I really need to answer that?' he said with a shake of his head. 'You were here last night, weren't you?'

Poppy's eyes widened and her cheeks flushed with that telltale crimson, showing embarrassment. It was so innocent and adorable. He balled the hand by his side into a fist, a way of holding his control.

'I meant,' she murmured softly, 'why do you avoid complications in your personal life?'

The question shouldn't have surprised him. He'd opened the door to it, by mentioning his usual prerequisite for relationships. But he floundered for words, strangely uncertain as to how to respond. Ordinarily, he'd have given some dismissive response, a non-answer, but with Poppy, the truth hummed and zipped through his veins, fairly bursting to be spoken.

He stood up, hoping that physical space might squash that instinct, but Poppy stood too, moving to his side, one hand on his shoulder, the blanket dropping a bit, revealing the delicate blue cardigan she'd worn at dinner. His hand had brushed her back as they'd taken their seats and he'd felt how soft the wool was, even as he'd fantasised about removing it later, because her skin was so much softer and he yearned to touch her, to feel her.

'You think that's unusual?' He volleyed back a question to buy some time.

She considered that. He really liked how thoughtful Poppy was. She didn't just blurt out whatever occurred to her, but rather took time to form her thoughts and express them well. Her inner lawyer, or perhaps what had drawn her to study law in the first place?

'Your whole life is unusual,' she said slowly. 'The way you were raised, the expectations on you since birth—'

'Not quite since birth,' he said with a shake of his head, then wished he hadn't interrupted, because his response gave far too much away. The darkness inside Adrastos that he preferred to keep all to himself.

'Since birth.' Poppy was firm. 'The expectations changed, after Nicholas died,' she murmured, 'but you were still raised with very clear ideas about who and what you needed to be.'

'Was I?' She was right, and he couldn't say how he felt about that, only that he *felt* a lot.

'Of course. As a young boy, an adolescent, you were Nicholas's spare, a backup. No one thought you'd ever be called upon to rule, and, as such, you were required to mute yourself, as much as possible, to allow Nicholas to excel.'

He made a grunting noise. 'Is this your interpretation, or has my sister been filling your head with this nonsense?'

Poppy's eyes held his for a long time, before flitting away, focussing on the moon across the wild woods. 'I don't think I'm wrong,' she said, eventually. 'Except you're not someone who is easy to mute.' The smile that touched her lips did funny things to Adrastos's gut.

'It must have been hard for Nicholas, to grow up in your shadow, despite the fact he was the older brother.'

'Poppy—' Loyalty, and his ever-present survivor guilt, had Adrastos's stomach churning. 'Can we save the psychoanalysing for another time? Say, never?'

Her smile was wistful now. 'Is it why you avoid relationships, Adrastos? Is it because you felt hurt by your parents? By them always wanting you to be different? Or is it something else?'

'Why does there have to be a reason?' He was pushed into a corner and lashed out rather than look at the horror-show reality she presented him with. 'Can it not simply be that I like sex?' His voice was far too loud. She flinched a little, but held her ground, and he fought hard to bring himself back under control. 'I like sex,' he repeated, and Poppy's eyes widened, so only an idiot would fail to realise that he was hurting her, and only a heartless bastard wouldn't care, but Adrastos was certainly, in that moment, the latter.

'I sleep with women because I enjoy it. Lots of women. And one day, if Eleanor fails to marry and produce happy little heirs to placate the palace, then I will do my inherited duty and marry someone suitable and set about impregnating her. Is that what you want to hear, Poppy?' His gaze narrowed. 'Unless, of course, you happened to conceive my child on our first night together, in which case, we might as well make everyone happy and just get married.'

She gasped, took a step back, and he could see he'd gone way too far, that he'd lashed out intentionally to hurt her and, instead, he'd said things that were cruel and unnecessary.

'I'm on the pill,' she reminded him. 'So you can relax. Neither of us has to go through with a marriage that we'd both hate.'

He scowled, glad to hear her describe it that

way, glad to hear her say that, because they would both hate to be married. So why did it feel as if all the gravity in the world had changed and was now pressing down on his chest, making it hard to breathe, difficult to see straight?

'Wonderful.' He grunted, his mood darkening by the minute.

'And with that,' she said, quiet dignity dripping from the icy words, 'I'm off to bed.'

He expelled an angry sigh rather than answer her, and a moment later, Adrastos was on his own, just as he liked to be, just as he always would be, if he had his way.

Poppy slept poorly. Worse than poorly, she barely slept at all. The entire night was spent clinging to her side of the bed, trying to keep her wits about her, out of a fear that her body might forget she was cross with Adrastos and her hand would stray to his side, would touch him, would pull him to her, would beg him silently to make love to her, to kiss her and tell her everything was okay.

But she didn't, and nor did Adrastos. At some point around dawn, she felt him move, the weight of the mattress changing as he pushed up and then strode towards the door of the bedroom. Poppy squeezed her eyes shut, feigning sleep. Evidently, Adrastos had no interest in continuing their conversation from last night; he slipped from the room without a word.

Good, Poppy thought to herself, rolling onto her back and staring at the ceiling.

She had a lot to think about.

Their conversation last night had given her no shortage of mulling points, including his insistence that this was normal. He'd experienced this sort of thing before. Poppy wasn't special.

She rolled onto her other side and now she allowed her hand the liberties she couldn't take in the night, reaching out and running her fingertips over his still-warm pillow, feeling the indent, as a sting in the backs of her eyes threatened tears. But Poppy wouldn't cry. She couldn't. To cry would be to acknowledge something far too dangerous to herself: it would be to admit how much she cared about Adrastos.

Which was a disaster.

What she needed was her best friend and a proper distraction. Reaching for her phone, not minding that it was still early, she texted Eleanor.

Can we spend the day together?

The response was almost immediate.

I thought you'd never ask.

There was a little love-heart emoji for good measure.

Whatever else happened, Poppy would always have Eleanor—her very best friend in the world. Poppy had to push Adrastos way out of her mind, and a day with Eleanor was just what she needed.

Unfortunately, Eleanor had suggested a shopping trip into the city, one of their favourite pastimes, particularly at this time of year, when they selected the gowns each would wear to the New Year's Eve banquet at the palace. Where they'd usually been able to slip out with a degree of privacy, that was not possible now, and, to Poppy's chagrin, the paparazzi scrum tailing them from boutique to boutique all seemed to want to harangue *her*.

'Poppy, is it love?'

'When's the wedding?'

'Princess Eleanor, will you be a bridesmaid?'

Eleanor squeezed Poppy's hand at that last question, keeping a blank face where Poppy was sure her abject horror must be quite visible on hers. They gave up after only forty minutes of trying on dresses, with Eleanor instructing the final boutique, 'Please send these six to the palace. We'll make our selections and send the rest back.'

Poppy was too shell-shocked to say a thing.

In the car, being chauffeur-driven back to the palace, Poppy turned to Eleanor. She hadn't realised how badly she was shaking until Eleanor reached out and put a steadying hand on Poppy's. 'It will be okay. This will die down.'

Poppy nodded, but Eleanor was wrong. At least, in theory she was wrong. If Poppy were actually dating Adrastos, then the media attention would only intensify. There'd be an engagement, and a wedding, and then pregnancies, all to navigate in the spotlight of this sort of media circus. How could he ever be expected to fall in love when this was his life?

'That was intense,' Eleanor said, perhaps just to fill the silence, or maybe to justify the sense of fear both women were feeling. 'I didn't expect it. I thought it would be like normal.' She grimaced, removing her hand. 'But this isn't normal,' she whispered, her own voice quivering a little. 'Poppy, what's going on with you guys?'

A lump formed in Poppy's throat. The outright question made it almost impossible to answer, because lying to Ellie was her worst nightmare. But she'd made this awful, awful web and had no choice but to stick with it. Just for a little while longer, she mentally added. The original plan had been to stay at the palace for the full twelve days, but she could leave early. Plead work deadlines and escape back to her own home. That wouldn't change anything about the faux relationship, nor their 'amicable break-up', but it might just spare her sanity.

'What do you mean?' she asked, not bothering to try to smile.

'Adrastos has never been with a woman for more than a week.'

He hadn't been with Poppy for more than a week really, she thought with a grimace.

'He's certainly never brought a woman home for Christmas.'

'That's not what he's done,' she said with a shake of her head.

'Nonsense,' Eleanor dismissed. 'You're dating. You're sleeping in his room. If things were as casual as you seem to want to insist, then why not stay in your own room and simply spend time together?'

Heat flooded Poppy's cheeks. How could she answer that delicately? Because the only silver lining in this whole debacle was getting to share Adrastos's bed.

'You know what he's like,' Ellie said gently. 'Which means you must see that this is very serious to him?'

Guilt was an awful, toxic taste in Poppy's mouth. She shook her head, wanting to deny it with the truth, feeling suffocated by the car's heating, by

Eleanor's nearness, by the lie she'd told with the best of intentions that was now eating her alive.

'It can't be serious,' she blurted out, finally, latching onto a way out. 'Do you remember the promotion my name was put forward for?'

Eleanor nodded.

'I got it,' Poppy admitted. 'I only heard on the day of our birthday party, and I was going to tell you straight away, but all this…' She gestured to herself, implying the relationship. 'There's been so much going on. The thing is, I'm leaving in the new year,' she said, so glad she could finally say something that was completely honest. 'And Adrastos must remain here.'

'Oh, Pops.' Ellie's eyes were moist. 'I can't believe it. The timing—could it be any worse?'

Actually, it couldn't be better. Suddenly, Poppy was desperate for the escape route offered by her new job.

'But long distance? It's not so far away. He can come and see you—'

'Adrastos has his hands full here. Besides—' Poppy worked hard to keep her voice light '—you know what your brother's like. I'm sure he'll replace me quickly enough.'

Eleanor's eyes narrowed. 'And that's okay with you?'

Poppy squeezed her own eyes shut. 'What do you think?' She sighed. 'I'm trying not to think about that.' More honesty! 'I'm just living in the moment, enjoying it while it lasts. Your brother is very special. I care about him, Eleanor. But this doesn't have a future. I wish no one had ever found out about us.' Speaking so frankly and openly was a balm Poppy badly needed. She was trying to simply enjoy things with Adrastos without getting ahead of herself. She was living in the moment. And she cared about him, a great deal. If only their one night together had remained their secret!

But what then?

It would have been the end of it. Adrastos certainly hadn't been going to chase Poppy up and ask for a repeat performance. If those photos hadn't been printed, they'd have been awkward acquaintances, instead of…instead of what?

She turned away from Eleanor, staring out of the window at the city as it passed them by, a blur of ancient grey buildings, falling white snow and the most beautiful Christmas lights still strung from one side of the street to the other.

Christmas was over, and now Poppy had to focus on the new year, and on the new version of herself. Once she left Stomland, she had to put Adrastos behind her, and never think of him again.

It was the only way she could move on with her life, as he surely would, the second he was at liberty to do so.

CHAPTER ELEVEN

IT HADN'T BEEN easy to analyse his mood that day. The remnants of irritation remained—had tortured him most of the night, and had lingered in the afternoon. And then he'd seen her stepping out of the limousine in the rather grand private turning circle.

From his vantage point on the second floor, where he'd been staring out of the window almost without seeing, all his energy became focussed on Poppy as she stood with innate elegance from the back seat the moment the door was opened, her slim body looking so vulnerable. He couldn't see her face, but a moment later, Eleanor came around to Poppy's side, putting her hands on Poppy's shoulders, squeezing, then pressing her forehead to Poppy's and smiling. Eleanor was…crying? And so was Poppy. Something in his chest split. A moment later, Eleanor wrapped Poppy into a huge hug and held her tight.

It was a hug Poppy needed. He could tell by

the way her body sagged into it, from the way she rested her cheek on Eleanor's shoulder and closed her eyes, and suddenly, the thought of Poppy needing a hug and him not being there to offer it seemed all kinds of wrong.

He paced out of the office quickly, took the wide marble staircase, then turned into the tiled hallway just as Poppy and Eleanor entered.

He stopped walking. Stared at Poppy as she stared back, and Eleanor looked from one to the other—but he didn't even notice his sister. Every fibre of his being was focussed on Poppy and her tear-streaked face.

'What's happened?' he demanded, pushing his body, lengthening his stride to reach her more quickly.

'Nothing,' she demurred, dashing at her cheeks and offering a weak smile.

'Don't say that. What is it?' Exasperation made his voice louder than he'd intended and out of nowhere, he remembered last night. The way he'd lost his temper with her. But it hadn't been Poppy he was annoyed with, not at all. He'd felt threatened, he realised now, by her questions and how honest he'd wanted to be with her. He turned to his sister. 'Eleanor, would you excuse us?'

Eleanor looked at Poppy then nodded, reaching out and touching Poppy's cheek. 'I love you.'

A moment later Eleanor was gone and all

Adrastos wanted was to scoop Poppy up into that hug he knew she needed. But standing right in front of her, it wasn't so easy.

'I—' she started.

'You're upset,' he said at the same time.

'Yes.'

'Because of last night?'

Her eyes shuttered, her glance falling to a huge vase across the corridor, stuffed full of festive flowers. 'Partly.'

He nodded slowly. At least she wasn't denying it. 'Will you come with me, so we can speak more privately?'

Some of the women he'd dated might have demurred, in the hope he'd beg, but Poppy was not like other women. She simply nodded. 'I think that's a good idea.'

He was relieved but also, suddenly, inexplicably nervous. He wracked his brain for where they could go—not his room, where the bed would distract them both, and memories of last night would be fresh in their minds. And not away from the palace, where photographers would be hungry for images of them.

Then, inspiration struck. 'Give me five minutes,' he said. 'Don't—Just don't go anywhere.'

The woods to the west of the palace were the only place Poppy had been told unequivocally never to go, and so she hadn't. Even though she knew Adrastos would go in with hunting parties, even though she knew they were simply woods, the warning given to her most sternly by Queen Clementine when Poppy was just a teenager had rung in Poppy's ears ever since.

So even though Adrastos was with her, as they neared the edge of the forest she stopped walking, hesitating, looking from the thick trunks to Adrastos then back again.

'It's quite safe. I'm with you.'

She bit down on her lip, wishing that those simple words didn't offer so much comfort.

She took a step forward, and another, and then she was enveloped—there was no other word to describe it—by the ancient wood, the smell of pine needles, the soft, fresh snow underfoot.

'Tell me why you are upset.'

It was a simple commandment, but also incredibly complex to answer.

'I—' She lifted her gaze to his. 'I didn't like arguing with you last night.'

His expression gave nothing away, but when he turned to look at her, she was sure she saw something like anguish in his eyes. 'We didn't argue,' he said throatily. 'I lost my temper, and I am very sorry for that.'

The apology was unexpected. Then again, why should it have been? He had been wrong, and he was confessing to that. Adrastos was nothing if not moralistic, and when he erred, he fixed things.

'Thank you,' she said, simply.

'It's not enough,' he said with a shake of his head. 'I lost my temper and you deserve to know why. The problem is, I'm not good at talking about any of this.'

She stopped walking, held out a hand. 'It's quite safe,' she said with a hint of a smile. 'I told you, I'm with you.'

His eyes widened and then he offered a smile back, the repeating of his own reassurance like an incantation, the bringing of a spell.

'You came so close to the truth of it all, Poppy. I wasn't expecting that. But I should have. You're so perceptive.' He lifted a hand, cupping her cheek.

'About Nicholas?' she prompted gently.

His face was grave; he continued walking—perhaps he found it easier to talk as he walked, rather than under the full glare of her watchfulness. Poppy fell into step beside him, reaching for his hand as the physical embodiment of her promise: *I'm with you.*

'We were competitive as boys. There were just thirteen months between us, you know, and I was always big for my age. We looked almost like twins. But we were not alike in any other way.' He shoved his other hand deep in his coat pocket, looked around, studied the lower branches of a tree they were passing. 'We were competitive, but it was never really a competition. While Nicholas was studious, bookish, he was also gentle and sensitive. He didn't like sports, he didn't like camping, hunting, any of the things our father valued. He would much prefer to read than run.'

'Whereas you were always the opposite,' she said quietly. 'I remember how strong you were, how big, how athletic, that first Christmas we spent together.'

'Do you?'

She blinked away, feeling as though she'd revealed something important, something she should have kept to herself, though she didn't know why. Sniffing, she added, 'Objectively speaking, you were a very sporty person.'

'Objectively speaking,' he repeated with a small lift of his lips. 'After Nick got sick, and grew weak, I felt this…awful sense of self-loathing. I cannot explain how much I hated my own selfish, stupid desire to beat him at all things. It had never been a fair competition. I had been born with skills he didn't possess and didn't have any interest in. I prayed to any god who might listen to let him live. I promised I would never gloat over him again, that I would never delight in my similarities to our father where Nick had so many differences.'

Poppy listened without speaking but, inside, her heart was breaking for the young man Adrastos had been.

'And then he died.' Such a small sentence to encompass an enormous amount of hurt. 'I hadn't realised how much I loved him until he was gone. Our competition was just a pretence to be together, to be a part of the same thing. I wonder if it was the same for him. I hope so—I can't think why else he would have kept agreeing to race me.'

He turned to face Poppy.

'No one ever asked me to mute myself for him, though, God, how I wish they had. I wish I hadn't been so arrogant, so desperate to prove my superiority at every turn.'

He shook his head angrily.

'And then he died, and life moved on. I became the heir, the sole focus of the media's attention.' He stopped talking, stopped walking, just simply stared into space. 'I was no longer in competition with Nicholas, but he was everywhere around me. Every article written about me carried within it a silent comparison to my late brother. And oftentimes, unfavourable to him, as if he wouldn't have been able to do the things I was doing. I was ashamed of my successes. Ashamed of any of the media attention

I received. I hated it. I wanted them all to shut up and write about Nick instead. To write how much he'd loved reading, how many languages he spoke, how thoughtful and clever he was, how philosophical. These were things I couldn't see value in as a child—but I had been a child! What excuse did these journalists have? Couldn't they understand how special he'd been?'

Poppy couldn't help it. She moved to him and lifted up onto her tiptoes just so she could place a kiss against his lips, just so she could show him what she couldn't say: how special he was. How much she understood and cared for him.

'You are special too, Adrastos.'

He shook his head, his frustration evident.

'I wanted, more than anything, for them to hate me,' he said, simply. 'I wanted the papers to write, *Prince Adrastos is the worst thing to happen to Stomland. If only Prince Nicholas were still here.*'

Poppy frowned, as something like a flame flickered in the back of her mind.

'You wanted their disapproval.'

'I wanted them to realise that Nick would have been a great heir. That he should still be here.'

'And so, while you couldn't change the skills you have that make you perfect for this role, you could ensure you didn't fulfil anyone's expectations when it came to relationships. Marriage. Babies.'

His eyes flared dark when they met hers.

'You've deliberately avoided relationships,' she said quietly, as it all suddenly became so abundantly clear, 'because you want people to disapprove of you.'

'I have no doubt that Nicholas would have been married years ago,' he said quietly.

'Oh, Adrastos.' Poppy shook her head. 'Poor Adrastos,' she repeated. 'Even then, no one blamed you for your love life. If anything, it simply adds a roguish charm to your persona.'

A muscle jerked in the base of his jaw.

'And as you pointed out last night, you have decades before you need to marry.' The words were wooden in Poppy's mouth. She pulled away from Adrastos, scanning the woods, which were dark courtesy of the thick canopy of branches.

'The thing is,' she said, slowly, 'I only met your brother once, when I was much younger. I don't remember him very well. But through your parents, and Ellie, and now you, I really do feel as though I have a sense of the man he was. I know he wouldn't want you torturing yourself like this.'

Adrastos's face was drawn.

'You're right. He kept competing with you. He must have known he couldn't win half of the things you fought over, but he came back, to be beaten, to be eclipsed. I think he adored you. I think he probably worshipped you a bit. Don't you understand,' she added gently, 'that he would want you to live your life without this guilt?'

He cleared his throat, shook his head a little.

'You don't need to atone for anything.'

'Don't I?'

'Of course not. You couldn't have saved him. He had leukaemia and he died. It's tragic and awful but none of that is your fault. Adrastos, listen to me,' she said, urgently. 'I need to tell you—' But she shook her head, because it was so hard to put her own feelings into words, so she sought instead to offer general advice. 'You are a wonderful person, and you deserve to be happy. Truly happy. You deserve a partner, someone you can love.' Her voice cracked. 'I saw that with my parents, and I've seen it with your parents. You deserve that. You're seeking to prove something no one will ever believe. That you're not a suitable heir to the throne. But you are. Single or not, you will be an excellent king. So why keep fighting that? I beg you…please, stop pushing women away in the hope you'll get some bad press. It won't bring him back.'

'I could say the same to you,' he said, after a moment. 'You have also made an art form of pushing away relationships. Our reasons are different, but the result is the same. You're seeking perfection and, in doing so, you've closed yourself off to the possibility of happiness.'

Poppy's heart twisted. He was right, yet he was wrong. It wasn't just about ignoring other possibilities. It was that there was only one possibility she wanted to consider.

She nodded in the hope it might appear that she agreed with him, but the realisation of how much she felt for Adrastos was detonating inside her chest, making it hard to breathe.

'I have never discussed this with anyone,' Adrastos said quietly. 'I appreciate how ungrateful it must make me sound. But you kept asking, and I simply felt—' He frowned. 'When I saw you today, I couldn't bear the thought of having upset you. I needed you to understand…'

She jerked her face to his then looked away.

'I *was* upset last night,' she agreed quietly. 'I didn't like how it felt to know that we'd argued, but it was more than that today.'

'Why? What happened?' It was as if he hadn't just bared his soul to her. Prince Adrastos was back, all mind-blowing control and power.

'It's nothing important,' she said, quietly. 'There was a paparazzi mob following Ellie and me. It was…frightening.' She shuddered. 'It made me very glad this is all fake,' she added for good measure, pleased that she could speak those words with such apparent honesty even when she now knew she wanted, more than anything, for this to be real. 'Because being tailed like that for too long would seriously suck.'

He didn't say anything, and Poppy didn't look at him. The air between them felt thick and heavy and Poppy's heart was hurting, but she didn't take the words back, even when she desperately wanted to.

'And then, in the car, Ellie had some questions, about us.'

'I see.'

'I told her the truth. Not the whole truth,' she clarified. 'But about the job in the Hague, and I explained why you and I would be breaking up soon. It felt…like a weight was lifted off my shoulders to finally be able to say something honest to her, and to know that there's light at the end of the tunnel.' Even to her own ears, the words sounded flat.

The air around them seemed to crackle and Poppy held her breath, waiting, wondering, how he would reply.

After a moment, Adrastos freed his hand from hers then brought it around her shoulders, drawing her body close to his side. 'Tell me about the promotion,' he invited. 'I'd like to hear what you'll be up to.'

It was an impressive opportunity for someone so young. Long after their walk in the woods,

Adrastos had been thinking about Poppy's work, about the Hague, about the role she'd accepted on the day of her twenty-fourth birthday. He was happy for her. More than that, he was proud of her.

But what right did he have to be proud? Poppy had achieved this all on her own, just as she'd always wanted, without letters of support from his parents, without the connections they could offer. He'd watched her working, seen her succeed from the sidelines and, yes, he realised now, he'd always felt proud.

Actually, if anything, he'd been in awe of her.

So why was there a corresponding sense of something dark spreading through his body, like anger and rage, all wrapped up in one? A feeling that he was being forced to walk a path he didn't want, that he was bound and on a track that wasn't his own?

It was different from the way he'd felt when Nick had died. Then, he'd recognised his anger and sense of impotence but at least he'd known why he felt those things. For Adrastos, this was harder. Nobody was dying. There was no grief to grapple with, and yet he was experiencing… the strangest weight bearing down on him. All day, and all night. Every night that passed, with Poppy in his bed, the weight became worse. They made love, and his body rejoiced in hers, his ego exploding at her obvious pleasure and delight, the euphoria he was able to give her and show her, the awakening of her body's senses. This was all *good*. So why didn't he feel that?

Nothing about it made any sense.

At the start of their Christmas visit, he'd just wanted this whole ruse to be over. He'd hoped they might fall back into bed once or twice, but he hadn't been prepared to lose sleep over it. It was only a fortnight, a little less, and afterwards, his life could resume its usual rhythms. A buoying thought, except he couldn't marry what he wanted now with how he'd felt then. Rather than wishing this visit to be over, he found himself contemplating the end of their arrangement with a distinct lack of relief.

And on the night of the famed New Year's Banquet, he wished he could understand the darkness creeping through his thoughts, the weight in his mind. He wished he understood himself better.

CHAPTER TWELVE

'YOU LOOK...'

Beautiful? Stunning? Perfect? All so insufficient for the vision Poppy made as she stepped into the living room, dressed for the ball.

'Too much?' she asked, running a hand down the front of the red gown.

He shook his head, frowning, still unable to speak. The dress had a fitted bodice and sleeves that fell just beneath her shoulders, at the very top of her slender arms, so his fingers tingled with a need to reach out and touch that creamy, perfect skin, never mind that he'd spent all night touching, that he'd touched until he knew her inch by inch, could recreate her body in the dark. The dress hugged her torso like a second skin, to just a few inches beneath her breasts, where it suddenly flared into a frothy but somehow incredibly elegant skirt, so swishy and...lovely.

'Adrastos? Please? One of the courtiers sent it over. I had chosen something far more...normal... I don't want it to look...'

He shook his head. 'Don't even think about changing.'

Her eyes showed doubt though, and he cursed himself for not reacting better. He'd been side-swiped by the vision she made. Ordinarily, he liked her hair down, loose in waves around her shoulders. He particularly liked it when it formed curtains on either side of her face as she straddled him, staring down into his eyes with an expression of wonderment…but tonight, it had been styled into a loose, sensual bun with tendrils loose about the face. Her neck was bare, and suddenly, Adrastos wanted her to wear something as beautiful as she was, something stunning and frosted like the snow falling outside their windows.

'I want you to wear this dress,' he said gruffly, closing the distance between them and lifting his hands to her hips, holding her there, feeling her familiar warmth through the fabric, 'until later tonight, when I will remove it from you.'

Her eyes widened, then a dimple formed in one cheek as she smiled shyly. 'Next year, you mean.'

He grinned back—it was the easiest thing in the world to do. 'Of course.'

'I just realised our "relationship" will span two years of your life—that's probably a first.'

She was right, but he didn't like hearing her

say that. He didn't like the reminder of how he'd lived his life before.

The thought brought him up short. Before? Before Poppy? Before this week? Nothing had changed, he reminded himself forcibly. Sure, this woman he'd been encouraged to think of as a little sister had turned into something else entirely, but that didn't mean *he* was any different.

'You need a necklace,' he said after a beat. 'Let me arrange one for you.'

'Arrange one for me?' she repeated incredulously. 'That's okay. I…think the dress is over the top enough.'

He considered that. 'There are jewels available in the vault. Come, have a look.'

Poppy hesitated a moment, eyes huge in her face, and then she nodded. 'Let's go and see.'

She had no intention of wearing any of the jewels from the vault, but she'd be lying if she said she wasn't excited to peep inside. The vault was a place that had inspired great games of imagination for Ellie and Poppy as teenagers—a place they knew they weren't allowed, *ever*, because it stored some of the rarest, most valuable jewels in the country, possibly the world. But Adrastos, as heir to the throne, and not being a teenager, Poppy thought with a smile, simply had to appear at the heavily fortified door and he was waved through. And then, through another door, and another, and finally, a suited man met them in a room with some gentle lighting above a line of wooden cabinets. In the centre of the room, though, there was a glass case, and within it stood crowns and tiaras, at least a dozen.

Poppy stopped walking and stared. 'Ellie should be here,' she said with a smile at Adrastos, and her heart skipped a beat, just as it always did now, whenever she looked at him. How could she go back to the way things were before? How would they interact after this?

Where usually certainty sat inside Poppy's chest there was only doubt now, a big chasm of not knowing. She didn't like it.

'I'm actually quite pleased she's not,' he drawled.

'Is there anything particular you would like to look at, Your Highness?'

Adrastos turned to Poppy, stared at her for so long her skin prickled all over and heat flooded her cheeks.

'Diamonds. A choker, I think.'

'Very good, Your Highness.'

'Adrastos.' Poppy shook her head. 'I wanted to see the vault, but I can't possibly wear—'

The man in the suit approached, holding a velvet board with a single necklace in the centre of it. A diamond choker, just as Adrastos had specified, and quite possibly one of the most beautiful things Poppy had ever seen.

'This was a gift for Her Majesty Queen Marguerite, in the late nineteenth century. The diamonds were initially the property of Queen Elizabeth the First of England. They were refashioned into a necklace as a gift for Her Majesty. Queen Clementine has worn this necklace only once before, to a state dinner. It is a beautiful item.'

Poppy couldn't look away from the thing. It was so much more than beautiful. Delicate, shiny, exquisite, and with the kind of history that made Poppy almost want to pass out. Imagine wearing at her throat diamonds that had once belonged to the famed Elizabethan Queen, a woman who'd known Shakespeare and was recognisable the world over?

She shook her head quickly. 'I can't wear it.'

'Why not?' Adrastos asked, reaching out and lifting the necklace without any of the awe that Poppy felt. Why should he be awed? To Adrastos, this was all normal. It had not been his birthright, and yet he'd assumed that role with the same effortlessness he brought to everything. He couldn't understand how, to Poppy, this was just a step too far. Their game of make-believe was getting harder to understand, the rules no longer clear, the parameters shifting so wildly.

'You know why not,' she whispered meaningfully, glaring at him.

'Please, give us a moment.' he murmured towards the palace jeweller, who bowed and left immediately.

'Adrastos, I wanted to see the vault, but not because I thought I would actually wear anything from here. These things are beautiful, but it's not my place to wear them.'

'Why not?'

'You seriously can't see the problem in this?'

'No.'

'If I wear that—' she gestured to the necklace, then couldn't resist reaching out to touch it '—someone is going to recognise it as one of the palace jewels. An article will run about me wearing it. People will believe that we are way more serious than we're pretending to be. And this is all just pretend,' she said, needing desperately to remind herself of that. 'If I wear that, your parents, your sister, are going to see it and they might think, they'll hope…'

'Yes, they'll hope,' he agreed, but with obvious irritation. 'It's just a necklace.'

'You know better than that. These jewels are all about symbolism, and the symbolism of me wearing one tonight would be too much. We're lying to everyone,' she said with a catch in her throat. 'I don't want to make this worse than it already is.'

He frowned, but evidently thought better of arguing. 'It's your decision,' he said, quietly.

A short while later, as they made their way to the grand foyer that provided the entrance to the ballroom where the banquet would be held, Poppy hesitated. She felt as though it were almost impossible to breathe, as though she could hardly speak, but she knew she needed to say something. Uneasiness was creeping into her veins, a darkness she couldn't explain but knew she somehow needed to.

'Adrastos, listen, about tonight.' She stopped walking, reaching for his wrist to hold him back with her. There would be people in the foyer. They had only a few steps to go before they were absorbed by the evening. 'I think we should be careful, with how we behave.'

'Meaning?'

She gnawed on her lower lip. 'In six days, I'm leaving the country. We've done what we set out to do. Your parents don't think we had some reckless one-night stand. They're not mad at us. But I don't want to give them false hope. I don't want them to think we actually have a future.' Her voice wobbled a little. Damn it, her emotions were all over the place. She forced a smile. 'It just makes sense.'

'Would you like me to stand over on the other side of the room? To ignore you all night?'

Was he annoyed? She couldn't tell. He sounded calm enough but there was a flicker of something in his voice that confused Poppy.

'Not exactly, no. But you shouldn't...'

'Shouldn't what?' he asked, eyes skimming her face, and Poppy drew a blank. Shouldn't look at her as if he wanted to peel the dress from her body? Shouldn't ask her to dance? Shouldn't stand with her and talk until she smiled, or laughed?

'I don't know,' she gave up with a shrug. 'Just...be careful.'

'Poppy, the whole world believes we are dating. To be seen together at the ball is going to reinforce that belief.' He lifted a hand, gently touched her cheek. 'Are you regretting this?'

She pulled a face. 'I regret lying to your mother,' she said, then wrinkled her brow. Because that wasn't quite accurate. She hated lying, but this week had been one of the best of her life. She would never take it back. 'I just don't want anyone to get hurt.'

He nodded slowly. 'Fortunately for you, I don't think anyone in the world has any confidence that I can make a relationship work. We'll part ways in six days' time, and all the world will know it's just Adrastos being Adrastos.'

He smiled, but it didn't reach his eyes. Poppy wanted to kiss him, but she knew that if she did all the tension and doubt in the middle of her chest would burst into something else and she might actually break down and cry.

'In which case, let's go, Your Highness.'

But his last statement sat with Poppy all night, tightening around her throat almost as if she'd worn the necklace and the necklace had been a noose. She felt it and, despite lifting her hand to her throat and pressing her fingers to the flesh there, she couldn't loosen it, couldn't make herself relax, make her breathing grow easier. She was exhausted as the night went on—not from making small talk with people but from being close to Adrastos and trying to get everything *right*. How to play the part of his girlfriend without allowing it to appear as though either had a serious wish for *more*?

Why did that matter so much to her? Why did she want to rail against the genuine expectation that their relationship might somehow seem permanent? That was obviously a risk they'd taken right from the beginning of all this, so why did it bother her so much now?

Because of the parameters shifting, she reminded herself, sipping a champagne just before midnight.

'Come with me.' Adrastos appeared out of nowhere, catching her hand, pulling her with him. She frowned, looked around, but everyone was far too merry and involved in their own conversations to care too much about Adrastos and Poppy. He pulled her through the edge of the crowd and towards a set of large glass doors that opened onto a terrace.

Just like that first night, Poppy's birthday, it was cold. Colder, in fact, tonight, with snow falling in swirls around them, and Adrastos shrugged out of his jacket and wrapped it around Poppy's shoulders. The hum of the party was behind them; here, they were alone.

'What are we doing?' she asked, her heart lifting, her stomach squeezing.

'Celebrating the new year.'

'Isn't that what the party is for?'

'Given our conversation before the ball, I thought you might not appreciate being kissed in the middle of the room.'

This was so ridiculous. Shouldn't she have insisted he kiss her in front of everyone? Wasn't that the point of a fake relationship? She shook her head slowly, a sigh strangled in her throat. It was almost impossible to wrestle with her emotions. All night she'd been trying, and all night feelings had stormed through her. Now she was alone with Adrastos, emotions were taking over.

'Poppy?'

'I'm sorry. I was just thinking how strange this all is.'

'In what way?'

'We're doing this to convince everyone we're a couple and yet I'm insisting we don't do anything coupley. I don't know… I've lost sight of everything.'

He moved closer, his body warm and big, his strength wrapping around her, making Poppy's heart lift.

'What have you lost sight of?'

She shook her head. She wanted to explain, to put into words how she was feeling, but she didn't have the words to properly answer him.

'We'll part ways in six days' time, and all the world will know it's just Adrastos being Adrastos.'

But then it dawned on her. Poppy didn't want to part ways in six days' time. She didn't want to leave Adrastos. Not then, not ever.

She pulled away from him, moving down the terrace a little, the din of the party just background noise to the frantic nature of her thoughts. This was a fake relationship, but why? What about it was fake? Not the way they talked to each other, not the way they slept together, not the way they just…clicked.

Everything about Adrastos was *right* for Poppy. It was all *real*. She gasped, lifting a hand to her lips and turning to stare at him as her heart went *kerthunk* in her chest for another reason altogether now. Relief that finally Poppy was listening. Finally, she understood.

She loved Adrastos.

Not fake love.

Real, all-consuming love. From the tip of her head to the bottom of her toes. *Love.* For all of him. The warrior, the ruler, and the broken, grieving brother. She loved this man, every angle, every facet, every part.

'Adrastos…'

His name was a whisper on the breeze, barely audible, but with that one word, she might as well have been pledging herself to him for life. Her heart cracked, because Adrastos didn't want that. He'd made that clear. He'd told her why he avoided relationships, he'd told her he didn't even care about producing the required royal heir. But that was *before*. What if his parameters had changed too? What if the easy, rule-bound fake relationship they'd established in the beginning had morphed into something else for Adrastos too? What if he loved her back?

Hope was a soaring light within her, brighter than the snow was cold.

Inside, the countdown to midnight began, a chorus of voices, happy and joyous, with no idea that, outside, Poppy was walking a tightrope, happily ever after on one side and desperate loneliness the other. For though she'd been alone before Adrastos, it was only now, in contrast to the way she'd begun to feel when they were together, that she would know loneliness.

'Ten—nine—'

Adrastos lifted a finger, crooked it towards himself.

'Eight—seven—'

And despite her fear and the doubts tumbling through her like detritus in a hurricane, Poppy travelled forward, one step, and then another—

'Six—five—'

He smelled so good, like citrus and pine needles, so masculine and so familiar, so she knew she'd never be able to walk in a forest again nor pass by an orchard in the summer without thinking of Adrastos, without wanting him.

'Four—three—'

His hand came around her back, fingers splayed wide, pushing her forward. Their bodies melded, so perfect, so right, so blissful. His mouth lowered and the air around them sizzled and popped.

'Two—'

Poppy held her breath, her toes curled in her elegant shoes.

'One!'

His lips claimed hers, slowly, gently, perfectly,

so the sting in her eyes gave way and a tear rolled delicately down one cheek as she tilted her head back, giving him access to all of her, kissing him back with the desperate certainty that she couldn't wait another six days for the axe to drop. This either had to be their last night together, or it had to be a true beginning: a new year, and the start of something new for both of them—a real relationship.

Cheers and crying and clapping came from inside and the strains of 'Auld Lang Syne' filled the air. Adrastos lifted his head, looking down at Poppy, eyes so beautiful and all seeing, a frown forming as he recognised the tear and lifted his finger to smudge it away.

'Happy New Year, Poppy.'

Her breath caught in her throat. She wanted to say it back, but other words were more urgent, more pressing, and instead she found herself just nodding, jerking her head.

'Adrastos—' His name now flooded her body with a powerful, drugging need. He was her other half. The perfect love. Just as her parents had felt that happiness and completeness, she'd felt it too. Here, with Adrastos. He was a part of her. But was she a part of him? Her parents' love had been a fairy tale because it was mutual. If Adrastos didn't love her back, then everything she felt might as well have been a torture device.

'Let's go upstairs.'

To his suite. She stared at him, the floor feeling uneven beneath her feet. But the idea of disappearing into that apartment was anathema to Poppy. It was another part of the pretence, and yet it was where their relationship had begun to feel truly real for her. Before she crossed that threshold once more, she had to know: was his apartment a stage set, or the backdrop to their real-life romance?

'I—Not just yet. I need to—' She bit into her lower lip, frustrated with herself. 'We need to talk.'

He was quiet, waiting for her. Not so much a 'we need to talk' as Poppy needing to talk to Adrastos. To ask him something important.

But how could she? Prior to the night they'd slept together, she'd had no experience with men in the bedroom, and she had even less experience with the emotional side of a relationship, with the vocabulary required to discuss feelings.

Just be honest.

Oh, how ironic, given that this was all supposedly fake.

'This is hard,' she said on a sigh.

'You can tell me anything, Poppy. You can say anything.'

Sure she could. But what would it change between them? Anything? Everything?

'I'm starting to have doubts about this,' she said, quietly. 'About the agreement we made, about what's meant to be the clear-cut nature of our "relationship". Things have become more complicated than we anticipated.'

His expression gave nothing away. The air pulsed with nervousness, tension, anxiety, but was it all from Poppy? Or did Adrastos have some sense of what was coming?

She took a deep breath. She had to do this. Didn't she? Or could she just pretend everything was normal? Stick out the next six days and then leave as planned? She was about to throw a grenade into both their lives, didn't it bear thinking about, at least for a moment? The weight grew heavier, the feeling of something being wrapped around her throat, and the words responsible, choking her from within, refused to budge.

'It doesn't matter,' she said after a beat, cursing herself for not being brave enough, while simultaneously thanking her lucky stars she'd averted a definite disaster. 'I think I'm just tired.'

His lips tugged downward and his brows knitted together, but a moment later her hand was in his and he was leading her to their room, not through the party but along the terrace and into a different entrance, so no one else could see the paleness of her face.

CHAPTER THIRTEEN

ADRASTOS HAD LITTLE time for indirectness. He appreciated the importance of discretion at times, particularly with regards to diplomatic discussions, but in his personal life, he always spoke clearly.

It was why he could be confident that he'd never hurt a woman with false expectations. Even if his reputation hadn't preceded him, Adrastos was frank about his situation *before* getting into bed with a woman. It was an easy enough conversation to have: a short discussion of his desire to stay single, to keep things 'light' and temporary, an aversion to future planning, to discussing anything overly personal.

These were rules he'd broken again and again with Poppy, but only because they had the broader protection of their 'fake' relationship and her upcoming departure to enforce invisible, important boundaries.

He didn't need to avoid personal conversations because they'd defined what they were doing at the start of this. She'd created the need for a ruse, and at first he'd been hesitant, but actually it was…a lot of fun. He'd enjoyed himself. He almost felt sorry that she was leaving in six days, which was exactly why he was craving the end to this.

He needed the simplicity of life pre-Poppy, the order that came from knowing he was alone, all by himself, and always would be. Perhaps it wasn't fair to put such expectations on Eleanor—maybe she would want to avoid marriage too? But somehow, he doubted it. It felt right that she should provide the royal heirs Nicholas couldn't, a way of sharing out Nick's responsibilities between both siblings.

He fell asleep that night with Poppy beside him and a determination about what the future held that didn't quite fit in his gut, but that he knew he had to stick to. Adrastos had spent a long time carving out a very specific life for himself: it was the only way he knew how to live. Nonetheless, perhaps it wouldn't hurt to clarify things with Poppy again.

Last night, he could have sworn she'd been about to say something. Something important. He didn't know for sure it was about him, about their future, but just in case she was starting to feel something silly, like that she might want more from him, it was probably a good idea to remind her that Adrastos wasn't the man she was looking for. In the morning, he'd make sure she understood his limitations. It felt important.

He turned onto his side, stared at the wall, and put aside thoughts of his own future, the life he'd made for himself, to imagine Poppy's life after this. To imagine Poppy and her career, her future bright and glittering, so beautiful and fascinating, compassionate, smart, loyal, kind. He imagined her leaving the palace, leaving him, and the people she would meet, the opportunity she'd have to replace him, and told himself he was glad: she deserved the happiness she sought, the perfect relationship her parents had shown her.

Adrastos would always be glad, though, that they'd shared this experience. Something had changed within him, and he suspected, he hoped, it was the same for Poppy too.

Poppy woke with a start as the dawn light broke across the forest, bathing the trees in shades of purple and silver, ghostly and ancient against the winter's sky. She stared at them without seeing, the beating of a drum sounding in her ears, before wrenching her gaze towards Adrastos, who lay sleeping, half dressed, in the bed beside her.

She had to tell him.

Every moment, every breath she took, without being honest with him was like a form of torture. She would have no peace, no relief, unless she did this.

With shaking fingers and a frazzled mind, Poppy slipped out of bed and into the bathroom, where she showered quickly then changed silently into a pale lemon jumper and a floor-length skirt. She finger-combed her hair over one shoulder then paced the foot of the bed, lost in thought, until Adrastos shifted, eyes on her, so she wondered how long he'd been watching her for.

'It's early,' she murmured, flinching as she looked towards the window.

'I can see that. What's going on?'

She stopped pacing and stared at him, her heart thumping hard into her ribs. 'We need to talk.'

He frowned. 'Yes, we do.'

Hope soared in her chest. Was it possible he felt the same after all? She dug her nails into her palms. It was cowardly, but she was glad to be able to say, 'You go first.'

He sat up a little straighter, skimming his eyes over her face then focussing on her gaze, so her stomach twisted. When he looked at her, Poppy felt as though he saw right into her soul.

'I've enjoyed doing this, Poppy. Pretending to be your boyfriend has been more fun than I thought it would be,' he said, with no idea how faint that praise was. 'I think you are a very special young woman. I'm looking forward to seeing what your future holds.'

Your future, not ours. Seeing, not being a part of.

She nodded jerkily, awkwardly. The hope in her chest ebbed.

'You are wonderful,' he said quietly. 'And you should be happy. I hope, after this, you find yourself more willing to take a chance on a relationship. I think you'll make some guy incredibly happy one day, Poppy, and I hope he'll make you happy too.'

It was the absolute worst thing he could say, though of course he didn't know that. But for Poppy, it felt as though he'd grabbed a knife and slid the blade between her ribs. She spun away from him on a sharp, deep breath, her eyes filling with stars.

'My job makes me happy,' she said, stiffly.

'You are a passionate, loving woman.' He spoke with his quiet, trademark authority. Poppy squeezed her eyes shut. 'You cannot—should not—continue to ignore that side of yourself.'

But how could he speak like this? So dispassionately? Without a hint of jealousy? When Poppy allowed herself the sadistic indulgence of imagining Adrastos with whichever woman would come after herself, she wanted to curl up in the foetal position and rock in the corner. Yet here he was, so blithely wishing her well with whomever she decided to sleep with next. Of all the insults!

And when they supposedly had five more days together!

Well, that was a hard no. Poppy couldn't do this. She was strong and determined but she wasn't so filled with self-loathing that she'd subject herself to this level of emotional torture.

'I am, however, glad we have some more time together before you leave.'

Again, so calm. So reasonable. He could speak of her departure without even a hint of emotion. How deluded had she been to think, to hope, that he might actually care for her? That her feelings could be reciprocated?

Poppy could only be relieved that she hadn't blurted out how she felt. That would be her secret, held close to her chest, something she never intended to tell another soul.

'Actually…' Her voice wobbled. She cleared her throat. 'That's what I wanted to talk to you about.'

She turned, faced him, did her best to breathe normally, to keep her features relaxed when inside she was a tangle of feelings and nerves. But this would be over soon. She'd say what she had to say, pack her bag and leave, and never look back.

Except she *would* look back because this place was her home away from home and his family was her family. But she couldn't think about that now, or she'd cry at the hopelessness of it all. Maybe it had been hopeless from that first kiss, from the moment they slept together. Maybe it always would have ended this way. She'd lied about the nature of their relationship to avoid hurting other people, but in the process she'd put herself right in the firing line.

Had it all been a mistake after all, just as he'd said?

Poppy had thought herself not a good liar. She hated dishonesty and always had. Yet, looking across the room at her fake boyfriend, she found her next fib came easily enough—a form of salvation. 'My supervisor emailed to ask if I could start sooner. They're desperate for staff to cover this case.'

He frowned. 'It's the holidays.'

She shrugged. 'The bad guys don't really care that much…'

He was quiet a moment. 'I presume you can email back and say no?'

'I could,' she said breathlessly, wishing her heart wasn't in such an awful state. 'But I won't. They need me, and I can't—I don't see why—isn't this a good thing?' she insisted with quiet strength, when she could think of nothing else to say. He stared at her without answering. 'This gets you off the hook earlier. I'll tell your parents about the job, and about us—how it makes sense to end things given I'm going to be in the Hague for the next three years at least.'

'Three years,' he responded, sitting up straighter, something briefly sparking between them before his expression returned to neutral. 'You didn't mention that.'

'I'm going into a division that takes on long-term investigations. My project is forecast to take three years. I'm supervising a team of twenty—I have to be committed.'

'You didn't mention this,' he repeated.

'Is it relevant?'

He stared at her as though she were speaking in a foreign language. Poppy's chest hurt. She needed to end this.

'I'll leave this morning,' she said quietly. 'And be on a flight out this afternoon, ready to start tomorrow. It's the way it has to be.'

'This makes no sense. You always spend the holidays here, the whole holidays.'

She blinked away from him, turning once more to the woods and craving instead the familiar view from her own room of the rose garden. There was too much of him in this space, this view. Too much masculine, wild, elemental power. 'This year is different.' Which was putting it mildly.

'Are you saying that remaining here any longer will jeopardise your job?'

She turned slowly, her heart breaking. 'I'm saying I've been asked to go sooner, and I intend to. Adrastos, think about it: if we weren't in a fake relationship, if we weren't pretending to be a couple, would you really care? Do you even really notice when I'm here and when I'm not?' She took in a deep breath. 'Of course not. Think of this as a get-out-of-jail-early card. I'm leaving, and in a few hours' time you'll be free to resume your life as though none of this ever happened. Isn't that good news?'

'Oh, Poppy, I'm so torn. Of course I'm proud of you, and happy for you, but I'm also—'

Poppy braced herself for what Clementine would say next, and the older woman's gaze flitted to King Alexander, who sat in an armchair, watching both.

'We're disappointed,' he said into the void. 'We love you, and naturally we hoped you and Adrastos might progress from dating to something more serious. We cannot think of anyone we would rather welcome into the family as a daughter-in-law, nor anyone better suited to the requirements of the role.'

Poppy's face drained of colour. 'I'm very sorry if you thought there was any potential for that. This job is important to me. Adrastos always knew I'd be leaving after the holidays.' She offered a tight smile. 'We would have preferred to keep our relationship private, but once those photos were printed—'

'Yes.' Clementine winced. 'Pesky invasive shutterbugs.'

'The important thing to understand,' Poppy continued with the lines she'd rehearsed, 'is that Adrastos and I have the deepest respect for one another. We're…friends, and always will be. But that's all.'

Poppy left the room a moment later, eyes closed, lungs hurting with the force of her breathing, but Clementine was right behind her.

'Poppy, my darling girl, just wait a moment.'

Poppy stopped walking, forced a smile, then turned.

'I just need to know one thing before you leave.'

Poppy nodded, thinking longingly of the limousine that would spirit her away from the palace.

'If you love Adrastos as I think you do, then why can't you find a way to make this work?'

Poppy stared at the Queen, pain lancing her. 'Your Majesty…' she murmured, shaking her head.

Clementine waited with the appearance of kindly patience.

'I care for Adrastos deeply, but we're not in love.' She spoke truthfully. After all, that was a mutual state, and her love was entirely one-sided.

The Queen's voice was soft. 'I've seen the two of you together. I've seen the changes in him, in just these few days. You're good for him, and I think he's good for you, too. Why on earth would you both let that go?'

'My job—'

'Is a vocation, and I understand, with you, it is also a calling, but this is your *life*, my darling. I swore at your mother's funeral that I would stand in her stead, that I would love and advise you as I would my own daughter, and I hope I've always done so. I hope you know how I feel about you. But this is a mistake, and I cannot let you go without expressing that.'

Poppy's tummy squeezed. 'With respect, you're mistaken. Adrastos and I are not as well suited as you think.' She reached out and squeezed Clementine's hand. 'Please, don't worry about either of us. I'm looking forward to the challenges of my job,' she murmured, truthfully, 'and Adrastos will probably have forgotten all about me by nightfall,' she added, lifting her eyes heavenward in an attempt at humour that she was very far from feeling.

* * *

Adrastos was so deep into the woods, another man might have feared he'd never get out, but not Adrastos. He had every faith in his abilities, but, failing that, he wasn't sure he particularly cared. He stood in the centre of the woods and stared up at the leaden sky, at the snow that was falling around him, and pushed himself not to think, not to listen. He didn't want to hear the car pull out from the palace, he didn't want to think about Poppy ensconced in the back seat, being driven—where, exactly? To her apartment to pack more things? Or straight on to the airport? He didn't want to think about her flight taking off, about her physically being in another country. He didn't want to think about all the things he'd so blithely rolled off to her that morning—her life post Adrastos. His hopes for her future.

They were all genuine, but this morning, they'd also been somewhat academic. Easier to discuss because the reality of that life had been at least five days away, five days Adrastos had intended to spend buried inside Poppy, holding her, making her laugh and burrowing deep into her secrets to understand every single part of her. He'd thought they had *time*, five days. It might not have seemed like much, but when you spent your time as intensely as they did, five days had seemed like almost enough.

Almost?

He ground his teeth, pushed on, deeper into the forest, through trees that grew thick and gnarled with age.

It had to have been enough. It would have been enough. But instead, she'd thrown her departure at him like a bomb and simply…left. Disappeared.

He would also leave tonight. He didn't want to be here without her. He didn't particularly want to face his parents or sister, or the void Poppy would leave—another absence in their lives, like Nicholas's. He ground his teeth, walked faster, harder, uncaring for the snow that began to fall heavier, his footsteps that became buried. He had waypoints to navigate this forest and knew he'd be safe. Safer here, he suspected, than out there, where he had to deal with the fallout of their pretence—without Poppy by his side. She'd never be there again.

CHAPTER FOURTEEN

BUT IT WAS no use. She was here too, in his home in the capital, in the kitchen, palms curved around a teacup as she begged him to go along with her ill-conceived ruse. She was in the air, in his mind, her fragrance lingering in some of his clothes, her touch like a phantom against his skin, so if he closed his eyes and imagined hard enough maybe, just maybe she would appear?

She didn't. He went to bed that night and woke reaching for her, his mind not cooperating with reality, making him forget, so he woke with the happiness of a man who got to reach out and grab hold of a woman with the power to make the world shimmer gold.

Reality though banged into him at the moment his fingertips scraped empty, cold sheets, an unrumpled side of the bed, Poppy's absence.

The fib had given Poppy some breathing space. She would leave the country on the sixth, as planned, and until then she could hide away in her apartment, licking her wounds, bracing herself for the magnitude of work required of her, for the post-Adrastos life she had to step into.

There was a lot to do, in any event. She had found someone to lease her apartment, so she busied herself with packing up personal items, boxing some for storage and others to ship to her new home. She didn't like to think about that. Beyond Adrastos, there was a lot in Stomland she would miss like crazy, chiefly, Ellie, and the King and Queen.

When she'd been put forward for this promotion, Poppy had consoled herself that she would come back often to see the family, that she'd take all her vacations here, so it would almost be as though she hadn't left. But the palace was tainted now, a poisoned chalice. How could she go there? She'd half be hoping to see Adrastos and half desperately hoping he was anywhere else.

Poppy squeezed her eyes shut as another wave of tears crashed down her cheeks. It had been like this for the three days since leaving the palace. She would be busily doing something, like an automaton, working away, and then a memory or feeling would spark and she'd be crying, paralysed and unable to do anything until the grief began to recede. Sometimes that took ten minutes, other times, hours. Poppy was not in control, she just had to let the feelings wash over her.

She'd never wanted her own mother so badly as she did now.

As night fell, Poppy, a captive to her apartment, knew one thing that would make her feel better. A go-to she always employed whenever life got on top of her.

Poppy was a runner, and she needed now to pound the pavement, to feel strong and powerful and in charge of *something* in her life. She changed into workout gear, switched off the lights to the house then peered out. Paparazzi hadn't been there for days. She pulled the door shut, nodded at one of her neighbours without stopping to speak and then ran, hard and fast, until her legs burned and her breath hurt, and she was so sore and tired that it was almost impossible to think.

Running was her salvation, but she suspected she'd have to basically circumnavigate the globe before she felt anything remotely like herself again.

He stared at the photo as though it had magic abilities. As though if he looked long and hard enough he could actually understand if it had legitimately been taken only the day before, or if this was a trick by the tabloids, designed to drive clicks and make sales. Maybe this was an old photo of Poppy? Because why would she still be here, in Stomland, when she'd told him she was leaving earlier? Why would she be a ten-minute drive away when he'd been torturing himself imagining the miles between himself and her? Why would she be alone in her apartment when she could have been in his bed at the palace, or, better yet, his bed here?

Why, why, why?

Cursing, he grabbed his keys, and without stopping to think through the wisdom of this, or to consider that maybe she'd lied because she needed space, space he shouldn't invade, he ran out of his front door and into the car that was always waiting for him.

'Take me to Poppy's,' he barked as a flash ignited through his window and he ground his teeth.

To hell with the press; he didn't care. All he cared about in that moment was seeing Poppy and getting some answers. No, that wasn't completely true. He cared, almost more than that, about kissing her until she agreed not to leave. This became his sole objective.

Poppy read Eleanor's text just a moment before a knock sounded at her door.

I thought you were leaving!?

She didn't have a chance to write back though. Moving through her home, phone in hand, she paused at the door, peeked through the hole and then pressed her back to the door in a complete fear response.

Adrastos!

Oh, no!

Oh, yes! Her body rejoiced, yearned to throw open the door and wrap her arms around him, but her mind, her sore, battered heart, knew that seeing him again would be a disaster.

'Damn it, Poppy, I can see the shadow of your feet beneath the door. I can *hear* you. Open the door before someone comes and takes a damned photo.'

Well, there he made a pretty decent point.

But there was no time to strengthen herself, no time to build a wall of defence around her fragile self. She opened the door and Adrastos breezed in then slammed it shut behind himself.

And then he stood.

And he stared.

And he stood, so still it was as if he'd turned to stone, and he stared, for so long Poppy felt as though he must see deep inside her, past her flesh and blood and bones and tissue and right into her soul.

She tried to move. She wanted to. But her feet were as stone-like as his body, so she also stood, and stared and ached, and needed, and longed for the way she'd been able to reach out and touch him whenever she'd wanted, for a few brief days. But it had left a lifetime of memories and she knew she'd never *not* want to reach out to him.

'You're still here.'

She opened her mouth, belatedly remembering Ellie's text, too. 'How did you know?'

'Is that really what matters?'

'It's just, Ellie…she messaged me too…'

'There's a photo of you running. The papers said it was taken last night, but I didn't believe it. After all, you told me you'd been asked to start your new job early. You told me you were leaving. I thought you'd left.'

It wasn't like Adrastos to babble, and he wasn't exactly babbling, but nor was he speaking with any conciseness.

'You said you were leaving.'

Her heart felt as though it had been speared by a thousand arrows. 'I am leaving,' she responded quietly, then expelled a soft breath. 'On the sixth, as planned.'

He nodded once, a sharp jerk of his head, but his eyes narrowed and his face showed confusion. 'Then why did you lie to me?'

'Apparently, that's what I do now,' she said, glad that her feet finally got the memo and carried her away from him, towards her living room. But Adrastos caught her at the wrist, spinning her back to face him.

She closed her eyes, his touch so incendiary her body began to tremble.

'Why did you lie to me?'

This time, a glib response wasn't going to cut it. She shook her head, words failing her, tears—so much a part of her now—shimmering on her lashes. 'I needed to leave.'

He frowned. 'Was it really so awful?'

She closed her eyes.

'I thought you enjoyed being with me. I thought you liked what we were doing. If that was not the case, you could simply have told me so. I'm a grown man, Poppy, I could have handled the truth.'

She wanted to repeat that famous movie line to him, because she didn't really think he could handle the truth in this instance, not the honest to God truth anyway.

'This was easier.'

'Easier?' he repeated, his jaw moving as he stared down at her. 'For whom?'

She blinked up at him, confusion warring with anger. 'I cannot understand why you are behaving like this,' she said after a minute. 'Is it your ego that's hurt? Your pride wounded? You cannot believe any woman would want to leave you sooner than you were ready to let her go? Is that it?'

'I cannot understand why you lied,' he contradicted. 'I cannot understand why you would choose to hide out in your apartment here rather than just be honest with me—'

'Oh, go to hell,' she snapped, anger winning, confusion something she could analyse and interpret later.

'I beg your pardon?'

She wrenched her arm free, rubbing her wrist to erase the warmth of his touch.

'Go to hell, Your Highness,' she corrected, storming into the living room and looking around.

Her fingers itched to grab something and throw it, an impulse that truly shocked Poppy, who was not, and never had been, prone to violence.

'Stop right there,' he growled, standing in the door to the room, arms crossed over his broad chest, so she realised she had actually picked up a ceramic vase. Her eyes were like flames, pure heat.

'We are having this conversation and then I am leaving. But first, I want to understand what happened that morning. No, what happened the night before,' he corrected. 'At the ball. We went outside, you wanted to talk to me, then you changed your mind. And don't say it was about the job: I know now that's not the case.'

She ground her teeth together.

'There is no point to any of this,' she said angrily, slamming the vase back on the side table and moving to a window. 'You told me what you want—I just gave you your wish a few days earlier.'

'At no point did I say I wanted us to end things then and there.'

'No, but you did want it to end. You wanted to get back to your life, for me to move on with mine, to find someone who'd "make me happy",' she muttered. 'Do you have any idea how that felt? To hear *you* of all people calmly elucidating your wish-list for me? How inappropriate I consider it for you, the man I lost my virginity to, to be openly plotting my next relationship?'

Silence arced between them, as fierce as electricity.

'I was not—'

'Yes, damn it!' She rounded on him. 'You were.'

'Well, so what?' he said, not moving a muscle. 'Is there something wrong with me expressing a wish for you to be happy?'

'With *someone else*,' she reminded him contemptuously.

'And this is why you left?' he demanded. 'Because you didn't want me to talk about our futures? About what life would be like after this came to an end?'

Poppy's heart, already so broken, no longer

seemed to exist. In her chest, where it had once been the centre of her body's functioning, was just a black, inky void.

'I want you to go now.' She stared at him, and all the love she felt morphed into something closer to hatred. She despised him. She despised the way he lived his life, even though, in a calmer moment, she might have conceded that she could understand it. But now, she was hurting and breaking, falling apart at the seams, and she just wanted him to go away again. This was a torment, the prolonging of an agony she'd thought she'd already navigated. She'd thought she'd seen him for the last time and had stepped into her post-Adrastos life. She didn't much like it, but at least she'd taken those first few steps and survived.

'I need you to go,' she amended softly, eyes huge in her face.

He swore, shook his head. 'This makes no sense.'

Of course it didn't make any sense to Adrastos. His heart wasn't on the line. His heart wasn't anywhere near the playing field.

'I don't understand.'

She nodded slowly. 'I know that.'

'I want to understand.'

She toyed with her necklace, a fine chain she'd bought herself when she graduated university.

It reminded her of another necklace, one far grander, that Adrastos had wanted her to wear.

But how could she explain any of this to him?

'Our relationship did what it was supposed to. There was no point prolonging it, and so I came home.'

'That's very logical, except for one point: you lied to me. If it was all so simple, why not tell me that at the time?'

She blanched. She couldn't answer that.

'Tell me the truth. Why did you run away from me?'

Poppy groaned. 'Please, Adrastos, if you care about me at all, you'll just let it go and leave me in peace.'

He drew himself up to his full height, inhaled so his chest puffed out, then spoke quietly, in a measured tone, that was somehow at odds with the emotions swirling in his eyes. 'Let me be clear: you want me to walk out of that door and have that be the end of it? You want me to leave, and let you leave for your new job, and we will never speak of this again? Is that what you wish?'

No, her insides screamed, but Poppy nodded, her voice quivering. 'Please.'

He glared at her, his nostrils flaring, and she held her breath, until finally he spun on his heel, stalked towards the door, yanked it open and left, just as she'd asked him to, and this time she was pretty sure it would be for good.

The car drove him through the streets he knew so well, black body, black windows, as black as his mood, and with each mile he travelled he felt as though his head were getting closer and closer to exploding from the ravaging, pounding of his blood, he felt as though his skin were being stretched and his mood becoming apocalyptically awful until he leaned forward and said to his security guy, 'Take me back.'

The words emerged as a growl, or maybe even a threat. Adrastos didn't care. He sat back in his seat, stared out of the window and tried to shape his feelings into order, and then from that order to form words to explain them to someone else. By the time he'd arrived back at Poppy's, he still wasn't sure what was driving him, and he sure as hell didn't know how to relay that to Poppy, but he wasn't just going to disappear from her life.

'I told you to go away,' she said, through tears, so many tears, so he pushed the door shut and this time did exactly what he'd wanted to before: he wrapped her in his arms, pulled her against his chest and just…held her there. He held her while she sobbed and he stroked her hair gently and whatever words he'd wanted to say still wouldn't come out but it didn't matter because she was crying and he had it within his power to make her feel better just by being there.

And he wanted to be there.

He wanted to *always* be there, whenever she needed him, and whenever she didn't. He wanted to watch her soar, but also to be there when she didn't, or thought she couldn't.

He just wanted…her.

'Poppy, I don't want to leave.'

She sobbed. That strange ache in his chest spiralled and he realised now what was hurting—his heart. His heart hurt.

In a way it hadn't done for years, if ever.

'I get it. I understand now. I understand why you left. Why you lied to me. I understand why everything I said to you was possibly the worst thing in the world. I understand now what I didn't then because I understand us better.'

'You're not making any sense,' she whispered.

'Yes, I am. For the first time in years, possibly.' He caught her face, tilted it to him, because he needed to see her and, more importantly, he needed her to see him, to see the truth in his eyes.

'I have spent most of my adult life running from relationships, running from the very idea of a relationship, but maybe that's because I had already met my perfect other half and I just needed to be brave enough to realise that? Poppy, you are a part of me,' he said when she stared at him in shock. 'You are inside me, all of me, you are the very *best* part of me.'

'But you said—'

'I said whatever I needed to in order to make it seem as though I was completely in control of things, as if nothing between us had changed.' He grimaced. 'Believe me when I tell you: I would never have been able to let you go without a fight. Not now, not on the sixth, not in a year, not ever. You are my love, my heart, my everything.' He kissed the tip of her nose, gently, achingly. 'If you left because you feel the same way, if you left because you wanted something you thought I'd never offer, then let me say this: I am offering you my everything and my all, I am offering you the rest of my life, lived with you.'

Her sob now sounded different.

And a smile broke through, then grew wider, and then she was laughing, crying, shaking her head, a beautiful, perfect, emotional woman, the holder of his heart, the keeper of his future.

How could he have ever thought he wouldn't want this?

Because he'd never been with someone like Poppy.

Maybe it was even why he'd resisted relationships. Maybe his subconscious had known there would never be another woman who could mean to him what Poppy did? Maybe it was all for this moment, this perfect, stolen moment.

'But my job, Adrastos. I can't—how can we make this work?' Her smile slipped and the sun went behind a cloud. He would do whatever it took to make her smile again.

'You've worked hard to earn that promotion. I'm not asking you to give it up.'

'But you're here. You can't leave.'

'I can travel. You can travel. We can make this work. Can't we?'

She blinked at him.

'Do we have any other choice?' he pushed, because, now that he'd finally realised how he felt, he couldn't imagine a world without Poppy in it.

'No.' She laughed again. 'I guess we don't.' Then another sound. 'But there's something else: I've rented out my place. Someone's moving in next week.'

'That is not a problem so much as a godsend. You'll stay with me, of course, when you come back.'

Her lips parted. 'Adrastos—you don't have to do that.'

'I don't want to spend another day apart from you. For your job, I'll make do, but when you are here, in Stomland, it will be in my home, my bed, my life, with me. Okay?'

Her heart stammered and she nodded, finding it almost impossible to believe this twist in her reality. 'Am I dreaming?'

He kissed her softly, slowly. 'No, Poppy, you're not asleep. We're both, finally, fully awake.'

* * * * *